Praise for the 13 Reasons for Murder Series

"…hard to put down and am keen to read the next in the series."—Reader's Favorite 5-Star

"Full of sass, good friends, and a bit of blood, this novel was a joy to read."—Julie E.

"…suspenseful, addictive…hope there are more books with this character."—BookBub Review

"I look forward to…learning more about Britney."—Studiohnh.com Review

"…oddly addictive…cannot wait for the next book…"—Amazon.ca Review

"…flows at a quick pace and leaves you wanting more…" —Goodreads Review

"The plot is fresh and unique, a nice change to read something a little different..."—Reader's Favorite 4-Star

"…well written and kept me on the edge of my seat…"—Heather W.

13 Reasons for Murder: Meathead

(A Britney Cage Serial Killer Novel, 13 Reasons for Murder #2)

Amanda Byrd

Blacksheep Press, LLC

About the Author

Amanda Byrd is obsessed with fictional serial killers. From Patrick Bateman to Dr. Hannibal Lecter to Dexter Morgan and every butcher in between, Amanda loves figuring out what drives fiction's deadliest monsters. When she's not busy writing, Amanda can be found reading, playing video games, or watching shows and movies like Mindhunter, Hannibal, and Dexter. She lives in Florida with her bloodthirsty, flesh-eating cat . And her husband.

Follow Amanda online: www.amandabyrd.net
Sign up for the monthly email list and get a free story

Follow Amanda online:
Facebook: Author Amanda Byrd
Instagram: amanda_byrd_author
Goodreads: Amanda Byrd
Bookbub: Amanda Byrd

Contents

One

I WATCHED THE MUSCLE-BOUND jerk as John and I jogged on side-by-side treadmills. John was talking, but I didn't hear him.

I was too focused on the meathead with terrible gym etiquette. He'd put dumbbells back or stop using a machine and not wipe them down after he was done. He was so sweaty; he looked like he just walked out of a shower and didn't bother to towel off. And all that nasty was getting all over the equipment he couldn't be bothered to wipe down. How disgusting. He could easily spread disease, and whatever other general nastiness he was carrying around, that way. The only thing he had going for him was that he didn't look like a 'roid addict or a meth head.

I hit the Stop button on my treadmill and jumped off, steadying myself from the weird feeling I always got when I jogged on one. I walked up to the meathead and coughed—loudly, without covering my mouth.

He dropped the dumbbells he was holding. "What the hell? That's gross! You know you could spread that to me!"

I laughed. "Honey, I'm not sick. I'm proving a point."

John watched from his treadmill, shaking his head. No doubt he was muttering something about "Why does she always do this?"

"For real, man, wipe the damned equipment. We don't know what you're spreading," I spat at him.

"Whoa! I'm a nurse, lady. I know how to be clean!" He sounded like the dumb jock in high school.

The irony of that made me laugh so hard I almost cried. "You? Nurse? You sound like a dumb football player. I'm sure your bedside manner is impeccable. And I wouldn't be surprised if you're not running around knowingly infecting women with whatever STDs you've got partying in that body." I walked away snickering.

John glanced back at the nurse. "You should see his face!" He smiled, turning his face back to me. "It's tomato red, his eyes are watery, and—I think you made him cry! What am I gonna do with you?" John shook his head at me."

I winked. "Take me home."

I woke up in John's bed. The sex had been incredible, as it usually was, and every nerve ending in my body sang with delight. I heard John in the kitchen, running water and scooping. He was making our lifeblood, coffee. It may have been midafternoon, but he had a night shift, and I drank the stuff all day, regardless. I hadn't heard from Julie, which meant she must've felt comfortable enough running the office.

How do people even wake up to the smell of coffee? I can barely smell it now, only hear it. John had one of those twelve-cup makers like I did. We'd been dating a few months, though I really wouldn't call it that.

Here's a little background on John and me: He's a cop; I'm a serial killer. Perfect match, right? We first met when one of the nosy-ass neighbors of Alex, the guy I killed last, called the cops about a prowler or something. My Jeep was on camera, so they called me to ask some questions.

Naturally, I lied about why I was there. Anyway, the man who was like a second father to me had a heart attack, and John was the one at my door to tell me. He was also the first on-scene when Melbourne Police called Tampa Police when they found Alex's body stuck to the tracks of a tank in a mud pit. I'm creative, what can I say?

Things happened, and here we are. Still, only friends with benefits.

I wasn't complaining. He knew how I felt about the B-word and how much I didn't want to settle down. I knew there were married serial killers, but I didn't want marriage this early in my life.

Plus, damn near every man I met wanted kids. Not me. I play myself as perfect, but I'm just as fucked up as anyone else—maybe more so—and I wouldn't want a child to have to suffer this cesspool of a society. And don't get me started on the medical problems

Besides, I don't have the patience or tolerance. Like right then, when I wanted coffee, which meant I had to get out of bed to get my own cup.

I sat up and wrapped the sheet around me like a toga and went into the kitchen, grabbing the mug John set next to the maker for me and filled it. Then I went to the freezer and grabbed four ice cubes—coffee has always been too hot for me to drink immediately. It had to be exactly four—my habit dictated it. As I put the cubes in the mug, I gave John the side-eye.

"What's that for?" He laughed.

"Thanks for bringing me some" came my sarcastic reply.

"Brit, haven't we been over this?"

"Yes, but you could have asked, at the very least, instead of assuming."

He set his mug down, shaking his head and laughing. He bent down and kissed me. I backed away.

"Man, that's *so* gross! Morning breath…" I grumbled and playfully pushed him away.

We went back to drinking our coffee and talking about what we each had planned for the rest of the day. He mentioned trying to stop by my house while he was working, if he wasn't too busy, to which I merely nodded. He was used to that from me. That particular nod meant *probably don't*. John watched me as I stared into my mug of black liquid like it was my own soul I was staring into.

"You okay?" he asked.

"Yeah," I answered, not blinking or moving. It took me another minute or so before I blinked and took a sip. I was running back through the events that brought me to this moment, in awe of myself and my actions.

You just killed someone, dumped the body in a somewhat public place, and now you're friends with benefits with a fucking cop! Britney, you glorious, ballsy monster!

We washed out our mugs and showered. I kept an extra set of clothes in my Jeep for post-gym activities like this, so I had clean clothes. John put his vest and uniform on. A bulletproof vest was so deceiving, but I knew what hid under it. He looked good in uniform. Not quite my definition of "holy hot guy," but it worked. We went our separate ways—me to my house, him to the station.

When I walked in the door, Minion picked up her head and glared at me for interrupting her nap in the sun. Oh well. I wanted to go see Osten and check in with him. Since I killed Alex, who was technically his employee at that point, he'd been different.

Then again, he'd also had a heart attack that week. The poor man. His wife was always traveling, and his biological kids lived too far away. We had a bond almost like mine with Minion; we depended on and thought the world of each other. He knew my flaws—except the serial killer part—and loved me anyway. That was true unconditional love, and it was all I needed, my biological dad included.

Two

Minion crunched away happily on her food while I cleaned some things up around the house. It looked like one of those typical single-person situations where they're out every night, clothes strewn all over—none of it clean—dirty dishes in the sink, the whole mess. It was awful, and I was ashamed of myself for letting it get this bad.

As I cleaned up, I thought again about John. I refused to call him my boyfriend, and we weren't dating, just enjoying each other's company. He was a good resource for information about the cases that might involve me, which is part of why I kept him so close. And like I said before, the sex was good, so why let that go? He also made an excellent gym partner.

It was just shitty that I got grossed out by the ginormous assholes who didn't wipe a single piece of equipment they used. I'd said something to one of them last night, and he acted like I was one of those basic bitches. I thought he needed to look in the mirror for that tiny dick he was overcompensating for. The whole lot of them do. There was about five in his crew, and I was debating if that were too many kills at once, if it might bring a level of attention on me that I wasn't ready for. So nah, it'd just be the one meathead. I'd have to wait a while anyway before killing him, considering we'd just had words, but maybe knocking off one of his friends first…

I pondered it as I petted Minion before grabbing my keys and purse before leaving. I got into my Jeep, pulled out of my driveway, and headed for Osten's office. I thought about how I'd get that whole beefy dude group's names so I could look into their pasts and do the right research if I really was going to kill more than one of them. I knew the people who worked the gym desk, and one of them was shady as hell, so I could probably pay him for their information.

I didn't want to make any hasty decisions, especially after the cops had at least looked at me in the beginning for Alex's death. Then they made John let it go. The case was still open, but not for much longer if they didn't find any more evidence.

Better for me, anyway. I could continue to do what I do, unhindered, for now. Sometimes, I caught myself wondering when I'll slip up and leave something behind. All serial killers do; it was simply a matter of time.

I pulled into the parking garage for the building Osten's office was in and parked on the third floor, same as his office. Someone in a vehicle parked nearby honked and whistled at me, but I kept walking, annoyed that people still catcalled strangers.

Entering the elevator, I let out a grunt of disgust and hit the button marked 3O. I guess it stood for offices since the elevator looked like one used for service, with doors on both sides. It barely moved, dinged, and the doors on the other side opened. The tranquility of

Osten's waiting room greeted me, along with the girls at the desk. Luckily, they were all on the phone, so none of them could attack me with hugs; I just wasn't in the mood for it today. I wanted to see Joe and make sure he was following the cardiologist's orders.

He wasn't in his office, so I went to the employee breakroom and grabbed a salad from the vending machine. It looked new; I wondered who requested it and giggled to myself. I had it sent over as a "gift" to the employees, particularly since a few had actually requested it. I didn't blame them; going to restaurants down here was asking for your bank account to be drained. I mean, salads ran a minimum of twelve dollars—twelve dollars! No thanks, and I wasn't cheap. Sure, my dad gave me a loan to start my business, but after paying that back, in almost record time, I've been self-made. Though I credit Joe—Dr. Osten—for a lot of my success. Had I not met him, would I have risen so high in the community so quickly.

This year, I wanted to sponsor at least one community event, and Joe was going to help me figure out which one, along with the mayor. She was actually cooler than most people said. Yes, we had a female mayor. Hell, I voted for her. I thought she was doing more for this city than she's been given credit for, but enough of my ranting. I grabbed a salad from the machine and sat down to eat as Joe walked in, saw me, and frowned.

"So, we're not going for steaks," he asked, faking sadness.

I laughed. "Joe." I admonished, waving my fork at him. He laughed, too, and grabbed a salad and sat with me.

We passed the time catching up and strategizing on growing my company; after all, I really did luck out with Julie, and I wholeheartedly believed I'd never find someone I trusted enough to run another office. I used Joe as a sounding board for a lot of things—except my kills. I could only imagine if he knew. He'd surely die from a coronary.

But he knew all of my outward flaws, from the anxiety to the anger. Not even my therapist could figure out the anger or where it came from.

As for opening another office, we'd decided it would be best to hire my own temp and see how that went. That also meant they had to follow me around the office all day. If there was anything that drove me to the brink of unnecessary violence, it was being shadowed. I'd have to suck it up and deal.

We finished our lunch meeting by taking Joe's blood pressure and hugging. Every time we strapped the cuff on, Joe became an obstinate child but simmered down because he decided he didn't want to die. By the time the girls up front validated my parking and I got out onto Ashley Drive, it was pouring. Typical Florida; it would end in about an hour, but during the rain, people turned into zombie apocalypse survivors who couldn't operate complex machinery, so I took Kennedy and Dale Mabry and Waters back to the office. They were bigger roads, but I had more room to maneuver around the zombies and make it back to the office in good time.

Julie was surprised to see me—it was close to four thirty, and we closed at five. I smiled and went into my office to set my things down. Before I could even turn around to walk out to the reception area, Julie was in my office excitedly asking what I was doing there.

"Breathe," I laughed, "everything's cool, I promise. No one called and freaked out, nothing bad. I'm here because I wanted to talk to you about opening a second office, maybe up by Northdale. What do you think?"

She scoffed. "You can't handle someone following you around all day to train them."

"Of course not, but you could run that office… I just don't want to give you up that easy. I'd rather you run this office, the 'main office,' if you will. Joe suggested a temp and go from there."

"I agree with Joe. How is he feeling?"

"Same old Joe. Wanted steaks for lunch." We laughed.

"I'll put an ad out in the morning, then?"

"Please. Jules, this is gonna be shitty. Will you help me when I start to lose it? By help, I mean call me out when I start to get mean or anything else I do that I usually know is super bitchy."

"You know it. Now let's get out of here. Cody and I are having date night, and you look like you need at least one shower." She giggled.

"I showered today, dammit. At John's after the gym."

"Oh, is that what we're calling it now," she chided.

I grabbed my things from my office, followed her out, and got into my Jeep. I turned to pull my gym bag up front and noticed I still had rubber gloves somewhat visible.

My worries from earlier returned: *All serial killers slip up; it was simply a matter of time.*

Oops.

Three

WHEN I BACKED INTO my driveway, I got out, gloves in hand, and put them in the hidden compartment where I'd stowed everything else on Kill Day. I closed the door, locked and armed the Jeep, and went into the house.

Minion was pissed. She screamed at me from the stair closest to eye level, the look of abandonment and starvation combined on her face. Cats were assholes. She always succeeded at guilt tripping me, though, and I should be modest enough to admit she learned well.

Look, I wasn't perfect in any sense of the word. I just worked hard and acted well. I hid almost all of my feelings; my therapist was constantly surprised by feelings I admitted I had. I wasn't the rock-hard bitch or peppy smart girl with no issues I made people believe I was. I was manipulative. I told people what they wanted to hear, especially if it was professionally related, and I pulled through like a Golden Gloves champ. As I said earlier, I had an inexplicable anger issue.

My therapist was pushing me to try hypnotherapy, but I wasn't sure I want to dive that deeply into my own psyche. Will hypnotherapy tell me why I killed, or why I was usually ready to fight at the drop of a dime? My brain constantly felt like an Atreyu song from 1998. For whatever reason, "Lip Gloss and Black" and "Bleeding Mascara" came to mind. Maybe because I loved those songs, maybe because something about them spoke to my blackened soul. All I knew was I had no intention of digging too far into my own psychological crawlspace anytime soon.

I fed Minion and went upstairs to change out gym bags and the clothes I put in them. The stench of soured sweat was never a sexy thing, so I always sprayed them with Lysol and let them dry overnight, setting the clothes next to them. I had a touch of OCD, sure, but nothing major.

See, I had issues just like everyone else. Granted, not everyone else was a serial killer, but most people weren't fans of germs. Walking into the bathroom, I looked in the mirror to see if I really did need another shower, like Julie joked. She wasn't wrong. I decided I'd eat something first, then shower. The real question was what to eat.

I ventured down to the kitchen, opening the pantry first. I rarely kept leftovers, so I knew I'd have to cook. I was in the mood for French toast but not in the mood to make the mess that required, so that left bacon, eggs, and hash browns. I cooked the bacon first, the hash browns in the bacon grease, then two dippy eggs. Yeah, they're called sunny side up, but I prefer to call them dippy eggs. I have my own vocabulary for a lot of things.

Once everything was on one plate, I went to the table and flipped through the day's mail. There was nothing decent except the Ulta catalog. I *loved* getting those. I wasn't big into makeup, but they had some killer deals on hair care and skin care. Sometimes I did go a little gaga for the makeup deals, too.

I remembered I had hot food in front me and ate as I browsed. Then there was nothing left of the catalog, and I still had food. There was nothing left of the mail, other than to throw it in the recycle bin. I finished what was left of my dinner and washed my plate, fork, pan, and other utensils. It wasn't enough to throw in the dishwasher.

Minion rubbed against my calves as I put the dishes in their places to dry. I finished placing them and picked her up, rubbing my cheek against hers as she drooled and purred as loud as a tiger. I turned the lights out as I went upstairs, still holding a happy Minion.

I turned my internet TV on, selecting the app I watch shows from the least. I was in the mood for fictional character who had the same proclivities I did. *Hannibal* seemed to fit the bill. The TV show was what I wanted to watch, but I was always afraid to fall asleep while I had it on. I watched two episodes, then turned on another app and that show with the guy whose whole family were actors and the cute gypsy guy was a werewolf. Something "Grove," based on a book. It was good up until halfway through season two, but I was that person who *needs* to see the trainwreck end. And let me tell you, it was almost as bad as the same guy's version of *Cabin Fever*. I was a believer in not messing with an original, with a limited number of exceptions. Those weren't on that list. I passed out with Minion still in my arms.

I woke feeling bad about hating the director's version of the book and another movie of his, but I didn't know the guy and his shit wasn't my shit, so I gave myself my usual mantra of I'm enough and I'm succeeding…blah, blah, blah.

I brushed my teeth and got ready for my daily jog when my phone rang. It was John. I let it go to voice mail and hit Bayshore with a vengeance. I felt something negative pent up, and it wasn't my need to kill this time; it was meaner. I sure hoped that wasn't what love felt like because if it was, that was something I sure as fuck didn't want to touch from residence in another country.

Fueled by uncertainty and anxiety, I beat my body hard on that jog and only realized it when I was in the shower afterward and could barely stand. I guessed I'd be wearing sneakers to the office and going for a massage in the afternoon.

When Julie walked in and saw how bad I was, she picked up the phone and scheduled the appointment for me with my normal masseur. She tried to take care of me, offering to make me tea or get an ice pack, but I wasn't having any of it. I was bent on doing things myself…until I couldn't take the pain anymore.

I asked Julie for some ibuprofen and continued to work. She brought me tea, too. I was lucky to have her and knew finding someone to do what she did—I refused to use the word *replace* because she was irreplaceable. Maybe I'd wait to open that northern office. I felt overwhelmed by the thought of it. I knew I needed to, but something wasn't sitting right in me.

I looked at the clock: eleven fifteen, which meant I had to leave in about ten minutes. The ibuprofen must've just kicked in because I was starting to feel like I might be able to lightly stretch before coming back from an amazing deep-tissue massage that would later cause me to need to soak in a hot bath. I rolled my neck, raised my arms above my head, and continued with all the light stretching a physical therapist would tell me—that's what Heather did for a living. On many occasions, she'd helped me properly stretch for my runs, or at least what she thought were runs.

I left for the massage place, having an amusing time climbing up into my Jeep. By the time I'd buckled myself in, my eyes were streaming tears from laughing so hard. I sure hoped Jules got a good laugh at my expense, along with anyone watching my inelegance. I was sure someone was usually watching me. I mean, why wouldn't they?

I parked and almost fell out. I was excited I'd be feeling better by tomorrow, even if the rest of today was going to, quite literally, hurt like fire. I hobbled inside, and they took me right back to the room. I even needed a little bit of help changing, but it wasn't the first time and sure wouldn't be the last.

That negative whatever I felt during my masochism this morning wasn't the first time I'd felt it. I knew what remorse felt like, and that wasn't it. I was bothered that I couldn't figure out what it was, maybe lack of control, I don't know, but it always led to this: I abused my body, went for a deep tissue, took a hot bath, and felt good as new the next day. Even the bad feelings and emotions were gone. Maybe I'd talk to a therapist; maybe I wouldn't.

Tony came in, and we chatted for a few minutes before I rolled onto my stomach and he got to work.

Four

I DIDN'T GO BACK to the office. I called Julie to let her know and went home. The bath felt good, as it always did, but something felt better this time. It wasn't my body; it was me—my mind and emotions.

It was all too weird, this emotional darkness and light. Where had that horrible feeling come from, and why was it always at random times? I'd felt stressed out before in college. Was this stress but that of being an adult? Did stress vary that way? I decided I'd call the only therapist on my client list in the morning when I got to the office. I drained the tub, dried off, and put pajamas on, not caring that it was only two in the afternoon.

Minion was waiting for me in the doorway between the bathroom and bedroom. She appeared to look concerned, but I figured she only wanted more food and her biological clock was a few hours off. I picked her up—it hurt—and held her. She could tell I was in pain, so she snuggled her little head under my chin and kissed my face a few times. She purred and drooled while I petted her, and we walked downstairs to get some snacks.

I cut up some red and yellow bell peppers and set the plate on the coffee table knowing the worst Minion would do was knock it off the table. She didn't like the smell of most of what I ate, but when she did, she was known to try taking it out of my mouth. I poured a glass of filtered water—the water here was hard and awful, so bad I'd considered a whole home filtration system; I didn't know why I still hadn't gotten one. I took some more ibuprofen and sat on the couch, turning on some new sure-to-make-me-cry-like-a-fool series on one of the streaming channels.

Only the first few episodes were available; some made me cry like a fool, while others were just meh. In all, I think I went through about half a box of tissues as I cuddled with Minion on the couch and ate my peppers.

Once the last episode was over, I opted for something else, something more fun. I switched streaming apps and let the stand-up comedians have free rein over the rest of my night. The tissues came in handy when I laughed so hard snot shot out of my nose and I cried laughing. It hurt like hell, my whole body, but it felt good to laugh so hard. I hadn't in some time. Maybe that was what was bugging me. When ten p.m. hit, I turned it off and went up to bed, making sure the house was locked before I went out. One of the neighbors had a break-in a few weeks prior. Not that I was worried; I had guns and wasn't afraid to use them. What I was afraid of was trashing the floor.

I woke just before six a.m. feeling great. I knew I couldn't jog yet, but I needed to do something, so I hit my usual route on Bayshore at a brisk walk, jogging for thirty seconds every so often to see how it felt. While it didn't feel great, it didn't feel bad either.

By the time I got back home, it was seven thirty. This walking thing was killing my time. Not that it mattered much; I did own Passing Through, after all. I drank some orange juice and more water before going upstairs to shower and get ready.

Minion tripped me on my way into the kitchen, reminding me she needed to be fed. Wow, I was so distracted I forgot to feed the cat. This muscle thing needed to heal and fast. Besides, I despised walking. I *loved* jogging and running, and they were the best ways to keep toned, even before hitting the weights at the gym.

I didn't want to bulk up, but I wouldn't have minded some shredding and as much physical strength as I could build to manhandle my kills. The added bonus to sleeping with Sweet was that he was a personal trainer before he became a cop, so I had someone who knew what they were doing showing me how to do it right.

Then there were those big assholes. I don't know if they were professional weightlifters or just overcompensating for something—there were multiple possibilities—but they were gross and rude, and I honestly wondered how they wiped their own asses.

I giggled to myself as I started the shower, then proceeded to pick out clothes.

I parked at the office around ten and tried not to stumble as I walked. Julie was laughing as I walked through the door.

"You hush."

"Brit, come on." She giggled.

I smiled. "I know, me in flats is the worst. I can walk in stilettos, any other kind of heels, and sneakers. God fucking forbid I wear ballet flats." The two of us broke out into hysterical laughter as I kicked my shoes into my office.

"Uh," came a questioning, distinctly male voice. I glared at Julie for not warning me someone was here. I just said "Fuck" for fuck's sake.

I coughed. "I'm terribly sorry," I started as I walked into my office barefoot, "I had no idea anyone was in here." I glared at Julie one last time. She hung her head.

I hung my bag on the coat rack, and the man in the chair facing my desk turned around. It was Sweet.

"Dammit, John!"

He and Julie both burst into laughter.

"Well, it's nice to see you two bonding over laughing at me. Why the hell are you here, anyway? You know how I feel about unannounced visits." My voice left no room for argument.

"I haven't heard from you in days. I wanted to make sure you were okay."

"Lame. Get out. And Julie, I can't believe you even let him stay!"

She sounded sheepish. "We were both concerned."

"Oh, this is bullshit. John, get out. I'll call you when I can gym again. Julie, come—" I thought about it a second, "never mind." I flopped into my chair as Sweet left, the door chimes ringing as he did.

Five

I CALLED THE GYM, knowing someone I knew would be working. He was and gave over the information for all the big meats who were part of the rude night crew. He didn't ask why, only said something about "someone needs to do something about them."

I stifled a giggle and thanked him, offering to take him out for drinks in exchange. He insisted it was unnecessary, so I told him to call me when he was ready to take me up on it.

First, I ran their names through my company database as a kind of double check. Two of the four were placed. One, Brody, at a local hospital, the other as a desk jockey for a college. Brody was the one I'd had words with. Awesome. Target acquired. Now to bide my time.

I hated waiting, but what was I supposed to do, get caught? No way. Maybe I'd stalk his friend and scare the shit out of him for fun or something, but people had already seen us go at it, so a bit more time than usual would have to pass. Dammit.

It didn't help I was sleeping with a cop, which put me in a whole new category of "person of interest." I had to be doubly careful.

The thought of Sweet set me off so bad, I stabbed a pen clear through a brand-new notepad. I made sure it didn't mess up my desk, and when I saw I'd barely left a scratch, I decided I needed a latte to calm down. On my way out, I asked Julie if she wanted one, and she shook her head while talking to a client.

I left and just sat in my Jeep for a few minutes, thinking about John. How was I going to calmly explain to him that I didn't appreciate him just showing up like that? Especially because he already knew I didn't like that kind of thing. Maybe at some point in the future, but I enjoyed my freedom, for obvious reasons. Then there were the not-so-obvious reasons. I enjoyed my life the way it was. I didn't need another person to make myself feel complete. Maybe I was overconfident, cocky even, but I really did feel as complete as I was capable of.

I started the engine and pulled out of my space, headed to the closest place with a good latte and an extra shot. Not that I needed the extra caffeine; I wanted it. I knew it meant I wouldn't calm down until later, but I wasn't in a hurry to call him, anyway. Considering the way I felt at the moment, it was a minor miracle that I didn't find him right then and proceed to flip my shit on him.

I would have stopped by his place unannounced later—after the caffeine and my rush of emotions had run their course—but he'd like that, appreciate it even, so that was out of the question. I wanted to tell him to leave me alone, but I also didn't want to give up the regular, amazing sex, either. I sighed and slammed my hands against the steering wheel. I didn't know what to do about him, so I pushed the thoughts into a tiny compartment in my mind for another time.

By the time I got to the coffee shop, I was feeling better, though one little thing still bothered me: Most cops had a take-home car; John didn't. If he did, it meant he still suspected me of Alex's murder and didn't trust me enough to leave it in his driveway with me there. This thought, too, was added to the John compartment. It was all such bullshit, and I started to feel like I was actually sleeping with the enemy. So be it; keep your friends close and enemies closer, right? I smirked at that thought as I pulled into the coffee shop parking lot and parked.

The place was surprisingly busy. I guess word had finally gotten out how great they were. Who else sold a large lactose-free mocha quad shot for four dollars? No one, that's who. They were fast, too, which made the place that much more appealing.

Walking in, I was almost run over by none other than one of that Brody guy's friends. That spiked my adrenaline. Just like Brody, he was obviously an all-around douche. He didn't even say excuse me; he just pushed past me like I wasn't even there. It made me wonder how he treated his mother—or his girlfriends, if he could find any dumb enough to date him. Wait, what was I thinking? This was Tampa: the enchanted land of bottle jobs, boob jobs, and frosted lipstick—of course he could totally find chicks dumb enough to date him; what was I thinking? Silly me. I scoffed and kept walking.

I didn't want any more confrontations with that group because if they actually did start to go missing, I'd be the first one the cops would look at. Again. Nope, thanks for the offer, though. I ignored the Bohunk and walked farther into the shop.

Being a successful serial killer was a delicate balance of pretending to be flawless and graceful and resisting the urge to, quite literally, rip someone to shreds with a fork and thrown their bleeding body into the bay to rot.

I bumped into someone in front of me, jarring me from my thoughts. I mumbled a "sorry" and backed up a little—I still believed in personal space. The line moved quicker than I expected; they must've hired more people. I got to the front and ordered my peppermint mocha quad shot with lactose-free milk and kept the whip. I ordered a regular white chocolate mocha for Julie because although she may have said no, but I knew she'd need it by the time I got back. We're a 100 percent caffeinated office. Coffee, tea, energy drinks—we didn't care as long as it tasted good and kept us moving toward the goal.

Julie was grateful when I came back and handed her the hot beverage.

"How did you know?"

"Because you're mine." I smiled. We giggled, but Julie's eyes were a little wide as she watched me over the lip of her cup.

I was finally feeling better physically, which was common when my mind felt like fresh shit on a hot summer day. Compartmentalizing usually helped, but for whatever reason, this time it wasn't working so well. Maybe I did need to go see my therapist, if only to use him as a sounding board. I sat at my desk, tapping a pen on the now-holey notepad, thinking. I don't know why I debated the subject so hard, so I picked up my cell and dialed.

"Dr. Benjamin Peterson," he answered.

"Hey, Ben. It's Britney. How soon can you fit me in?"

"Well hello to you, too, Brit. You okay?"

"I'm not really sure. I've got something bugging me, and I need a sounding board."

"What about dinner tonight? Or is it something you need to come into the office for?"

"Dinner works. Where and when?"

"Six at the Indian place on Waters?"

"You sure know how to pick them." I laughed. I could never remember the name of the place, but it was better than that vegan place that paraded as an Indian restaurant. Tonight, I'd eat better than I had in weeks.

Six

JULIE LEFT AT FIVE, which gave me the time I needed to pull up the database information undisturbed on Brody and his jackass friends. I only had the two, but I got addresses, phone numbers, and emergency contacts. I wanted to scare those assholes. But how? Fake blood and bash in a fender? Sure, I was good at killing and getting away with it, though last time was a narrow miss, but playing pranks wasn't something I was all that good at. To be completely honest, I sucked at it my entire life. My friends were always better at it than me. Sarah would be the one to go to for this; she was the queen prankster and maybe a bit of a pyromaniac. I really wasn't about to get anyone else involved; that would be like having a kill partner. Absolutely not. Too many have been caught for less, and I didn't feel like I was done.

No pranks. Maybe some light stalking. Then again, that could lead right back to me. I really needed to stop being the last person to have a confrontation with these meatballs. With any kill, really. I didn't want another Alex on my hands, and I was starting to allow myself to believe John still suspected me.

Would I have to give in to the whole girlfriend thing just to throw him off? I hoped not, the thought making my stomach churn. I'd still have to sneak out to kill, and I knew he had cameras, so that was, without a doubt, *not* happening. I didn't want to give him any more reason to go prying into my personal life and background, which I'm sure he kept trying to do. Good thing I hid my guilt well. So well, in fact, that even a few psychiatrists determined I had PTSD from the incidents. Hah! If they only knew.

I looked at the clock on the computer monitor: 5:45. I had to go. I closed all the programs and hit the Update and Restart button before grabbing my bag. I didn't have to rush; the place was only a few miles east.

I arrived before Ben, and they seated me. I ordered a beer I'd never tried before while I waited. I always felt like a dick when I couldn't pronounce what it was I wanted because of my own cultural ignorance, but they seemed to understand. I always felt like they were calling me an ignorant American behind my back, though. I legitimately felt bad about it. I'd eventually learn new languages and fully experience other cultures, but now wasn't the time. I was still growing Passing Through and needed more Julies before I'd feel comfortable enough to travel internationally.

Ben walked in and spotted me immediately. I wasn't hard to miss—I was the only one there. He walked over and signaled the server for what I was drinking. I stood up and hugged him, and we both sat down.

"So, what's the emergency?"

"Well, I don't know. I'm sleeping with this cop, right? He thought I killed that employee of Joe's but couldn't prove it. Now I'm sleeping with him. Sure, I think I forgave him, but I don't think I trust him fully. Every other cop on the force has a take-home vehicle—"

The server came over with Ben's beer and asked for our orders. I got the lamb, Ben the chicken.

"As I was saying, the rest have take-home cars. He doesn't. And he's got cameras everywhere in and around his house. I'm not saying he doesn't trust me, but how do I know he's not watching the recordings from when I stay over to see if I've left because he, for whatever reason, thinks I'm a killer?"

That was a lot for me to let out in one breath. Ben grasped it all, though, like every other time. He sipped his beer thoughtfully and looked at me, almost sizing me up.

"Brit, are you starting to fall for this guy?"

"What? NO! I'd kill him if I could get away with it. He's annoying, but the sex is worth it, so…"

Ben laughed. "You sound so much like a guy."

I raised my glass in toast to that.

We went back and forth until the food came out, at which point we concluded I had a decision to make: Did I want to keep up the good sex or back off now before he got too attached and I screwed him over harder than anything he'd ever felt before?

Well, shit. When I thought about it like that, I felt bad. I didn't want to break the guy's heart, but if he grew too attached or too distrusting, I'd have to. But how the hell do you screw over a cop who already thinks you committed murder?

We ate in silence. I pondered how to gently let Sweet down, if it came to it, while also floating off into la-la land with thoughts of his beaten and bloody body on my hands—literally. I'd only kill him if I had to, and it seemed more likely that I would have to. That wasn't good.

We'd only been messing around a few months, but I knew he still thought I killed Alex, yet he was supposedly ready to start an actual relationship. Maybe he was the best cop in Tampa history and was playing the long game on me. I nearly choked on a piece of lamb, suddenly feeling like I was physically pinned between the proverbial rock and a hard place—just add a panic attack to that. I managed to swallow my food and chugged my beer to help wash it the rest of the way down. Tears were streaming down my face from choking, but I was laughing. Ben laughed too.

"Damn, man. I really need to chew first."

Over the rest of dinner, we talked about how he was doing, and he poked at what I wanted to do with my company. I told him the thoughts I had about opening another office and the doubts that coincided.

"What is it you truly want with your business?" he asked.

My face screwed up in confusion.

"Are you *really* asking me this? You fucking know what I want. I want to be the one every top business in the city comes to for people," I huffed.

Ben smiled, cool as ice. "What I'm trying to get out of you is recognition–acceptance–that you need to think this decision through. That it's not something to take lightly."

He made sense. Owning a business was like a deep relationship. In my case, it was my child, and I needed to do all I could to protect that child before I had another. I shivered as I made that comparison in my head.

Ben laughed, knowing I must've made some kind of reference that would usually make me throw up. Lucky for both of us, I didn't puke.

We finished dinner, and I thanked him for being available, quite literally, every time I needed to talk. This is why he made the money he did.

One hundred fifty dollars an hour wasn't enough to stop me from killing people, though. I was sure if I confessed to Ben that I was a serial killer, he'd think I was joking, then take me in for studies since I do actually have empathy—most of us don't. We can act like we do, but mine is genuine, usually, which makes me the anomaly I sort of am. We all have our burdens to bear.

Seven

On the drive home, I contemplated, again, opening a new office. By the time I'd backed into my driveway, I decided it wasn't the time. I needed a few more months, maybe, before Julie and I were both comfortable. I knew, too, that the more we talked about it, the better we'd feel. But for now, it was just that: talk.

Minion screamed at me and rubbed up against me until she smelled the curry, then took off into the kitchen, bent on outrunning the smell. I laughed and followed her—I needed to feed her anyway.

Once Minion was taken care of, I went upstairs to change for a jog. I needed to clear my head and also make sure I was doing the right thing about Sweet. He was a good guy who wanted to do good. I just couldn't shake the feeling that he still thought I was a killer. And if he did, I had a big problem on my hands.

I locked the door and jogged off, thinking what my options would be if I broke it off with him. I could start sleeping with his boss, maybe? Or get a restraining order? I didn't want to go to extremes; that would make me look guilty. I was starting to think that it didn't matter what I did; he'd keep trying to pin it on me.

I'd landed myself on a slippery slope, and now I was sliding down. I was on my ass, and it felt like ten miles of rocky terrain still to go.

Then I saw a branch and reached out. My jog had taken me to Soho. A bar, to be exact. One John and I frequented. That reminded me: I had to stay with him until he slipped up.

As for me, well, I'd make extra sure I wasn't followed. I vowed to check my purse, Jeep, phone, and a few other things for tracking devices, cameras, and any other way John could monitor my activity. If I did manage to find anything, I would definitely go to his place unannounced, but with a reason more than "I missed you."

What kind of person could tell someone they were falling for them yet monitor them like a felon? That wasn't love. Not by a long shot. More like abuse, and I didn't tolerate that well, whether it was me or someone else. And I'd be damned if I'd ever make someone else feel like I was the abuser.

I went into the bar for some water, and whom did my sweaty blue eyes see? None other than John Sweet. Awesome; he saw me, too. Now I was actually mad. I'd gone for a run that unconsciously brought me right into his waiting arms. Gross.

He waved me over and I wasn't going to be rude, so I signaled the bartender for a water and pointed to John. The bartender got my meaning and set the bottle down in front of him as I walked over. He was with one of his work buddies I'd never met before. If he introduced me as his girlfriend, I'd probably stab him with a straw. Fortunately for both of us, he didn't. However, the tone in the word *friend* gave it away.

I punched him playfully in the arm. "You can just tell him we're sleeping together. It's no big deal." I extended my hand to his friend, making him cognizant of who, exactly, I was. If he knew Sweet thought I killed Alex, he'd know my name. Apparently, he didn't know, or he hid it very well.

He shook back, telling me his name was Bobby. I'd forget in less than an hour, anyway. I simply didn't care who he was. He hopefully didn't know about me until right this minute, which made it easier for me. He offered nothing to me and so meant nothing to me.

I drank my water while the two of them talked, attempted to pay, but was shaken off by the bartender. I said bye to John and Bobby and jogged home. By the time I walked through my front door, I had four texts and three voice mails from John. He was upset I barely spoke and then left the way I did.

I put my phone on the charger and showered, coming back to more messages. I replied to him, and in a tone that conveyed how happy I was not.

"Why are you so annoying right now? I'm home and going to bed. Talk tomorrow."

I waited for a reply and got none, letting out a huge sigh. I was annoyed and relieved; he was starting to act like a jealous boyfriend, and he knew how much I hated that. I'd deal with him tomorrow. Tonight was a night for digging: digging into lives and dump sites.

I killed my laptop battery twice looking into that Brody douche and a body-dump site. I found the dump site a whole lot easier than looking into dude's life. Brody Rogers, thirty-one, single, six feet seven inches, and 360 pounds. The man was a beast, but a douchey beast.

Every time I saw the guy, I envisioned him using one of those grabber things to wipe his ass and about peed myself laughing. I just don't get why people with normal jobs—who *aren't* bodybuilders by profession—get that big. I never understood it. I never found it cute or sexy, but some women apparently did, which confused me even more. The only things I could think of were that he made them feel safe, or they honestly believed they had the guy all the girls wanted. I felt the bile rise in the back of my throat as I chewed on the thought.

By the time I lay down for what would now be a nap before work, I had Brody's home address and knew his rotating schedule at the hospital. Following him at the hospital would be the hardest part of the whole thing. There were cameras everywhere, not to mention security.

Scoping for fun was not on the menu now. Joy. I loved nothing more than hanging out in my Jeep for hours people watching. I mean, yeah, that was fun, but not in a dead hospital employee parking garage. It was dull and I couldn't afford to read; taking my eyes away for even one second could cause me to miss something, and that wasn't happening. I'd need more than a case of energy drinks for this, but I was ready. *The night would fall soon enough*, I caught myself thinking as I drifted off.

Eight

By the end of the week, I was ready to get the first of the garage-watching done. I was stocked up on various flavors of sugar-free Monster and instant coffee. I always carried a case of water in the back of my Jeep, had a power converter and an electric kettle. Instant coffee was the best way to get that extra edge—almost like liquid crack. It tasted awful, but I didn't have much of a choice. I needed to be in my vehicle at all times. This was going to be interesting.

It was still early, six p.m., but I was already itchy to get started. I needed to wait about three more hours to leave, when there was less traffic on the way there and when there'd be less movement in and out of the employee lot.

Brody's shift started at eleven, so I wanted to get there early to scope out where his usual parking spot was and if I could see him from there. I wanted eyes *in* the hospital, too, but that would require prosthetics, and was that a game I was willing to play? It was sure one I'd have to think about playing. I knew nothing about prosthetics, and those I knew who did lived multiple states away. Skype tutorials?

YouTube? I'd think about it, but there had to be another way—without getting anyone else involved.

I paced the house, tried to watch some Netflix, even tried to laugh with the B-horror that usually worked. Not this time. I was too excited—too excited to be going to sit in my Jeep for twelve-plus hours. This was the part of the stalking I hated. It was like police stakeout in a movie but one that sucked mainly because you were alone.

If I could get through tonight, I could get through the rest of the nights I'd have to do it until I knew the time was right. The first night was always the hardest. It always made me doubt myself. Hell, there were plenty of times I'd almost gotten caught, but I supposed luck was on my side because I'd dodged my target. Tonight was no different: full of doubt and impatience. It was one of those things I'd always felt and knew I'd continue to feel with each kill. It was a lot like Impostor Syndrome, and to a degree, I wondered if I was an impostor. Did Dahmer or Gacy ever feel this way pre-kill?

I looked at the clock, and it was only eight. Had I spent that long pacing, lost in my own thoughts and doubt? Wow. That was impressive. I'd never really done that for the stalk before; that was usually during the kill planning stages. Was I losing it? I shook my head to clear the negative out, but I still felt doubt—I always would, and I had to accept that. I decided to lie on the couch and maybe nap since I'd be up all night and longer.

I woke to a clock reading ten p.m. Oops. I overslept, so
now it was time to speed a little and hope I'd beat Brody
there. With any luck, I would—without a speeding
ticket. I grabbed my bag of supplies and headed out.
Minion screamed at me and gave me a dirty look,
clearly unhappy with my plans for the evening. I yelled
"I love you!" as I closed and locked the door behind
me and jogged to my Jeep. I climbed up and into
it, tossing the bag in the back, and drove out of my
neighborhood like usual until I hit Bayshore. Then I
pressed a little harder on the pedal until I got to the
interstate. I opened her up and managed to back my
way into a decent spot within fifteen minutes. It was
like the universe had my back or something; there was
no traffic, and I hit all greens.

Brody pulled up in a jacked-up pickup, blaring some
rock song I couldn't understand until he drove closer,
presumably looking for a spot, when I ducked down. It
was Five Finger Death Punch's "Burn Motherfucker." No
surprise there. It was actually a good song. I even had
it on a playlist or two.

He passed me without noticing I was in the Jeep and
parked in the outer edge diagonal from me. I could see
his truck and the employee entrance. I'd picked a great
spot. Now to note the spot number so I could continue
to park here and watch.

I'd counted six cameras on the concrete roof and two
by the doors. This wouldn't be the place I killed or
took him from. I was already thinking of where the kill

would take place. The body dump had been chosen long before the stalk was planned. I was anal that way. I wanted the dump site lined up even before I chose a kill site or method. When I was younger, most of it was more on the impulsive side. I tended to follow my victims and they'd… Well, that's another story for another time.

Brody went inside, and I began my hours alone, alternating listening to music on my phone and drinking nasty instant coffee or pounding energy drinks like they were shots at a bar. There were fewer cars in the lot than when I'd arrived, making it more likely for me to be seen squatting to pee behind one of them.

What annoyed me most was all the time I had to be inside my own head. Being confronted by things I'd carefully packed away, like what to do about John, pecked at their boxes like ravens tapping on Poe's window. I did my best to force the pecking to cease by ignoring it, though I knew I couldn't forever. I'd eventually have to address the feelings that John had and whether or not he still thought I was a killer. Maybe I wouldn't have to, though. Maybe Brody's murder would make him think otherwise. I mean, I was sure I'd found something documented in my own files where he'd had altercations with other employees of where I placed him. A slick grin spread on my face. Maybe this would be more fun than killing usually was.

Nine

Hours went by, and I hadn't seen a soul. It was five a.m. I'd polished off three energy drinks and none of that awful coffee yet, but I really had to pee. Good thing I was prepared for that, too. I'd be the first to admit I was curious about many pigs it would take to eat a guy Brody's size in about eight to ten hours. The answer was a dozen or so pigs. I'd totally looked it up.

By five fifteen, the first employee walked out. It wasn't Brody, but there were more behind the first guy. I ducked back down as far as I could go—one of the people leaving was parked next to me. When they left, I stayed down for a few more minutes until I heard arguing. I crept up and looked around. It was Brody. He was on the phone yelling at someone, threatening to kill them. Because that's how you won an argument. What a jackass. Once I was able to recall who he was, I couldn't recall him being particularly articulate when he worked for me. He muttered another threat and went back inside. Man, that dude had an anger issue. That made me wonder if he had an injectables issue, too.

I sat back up, made a note to look into whom he was threatening and why, and went back to waiting. I didn't think blackmail or anything like that. It was probably over money owed to him. More digging that was a little more difficult. I liked a challenge; it let me know how good I was and what I needed to work on.

The rest of the time passed uneventfully, and when ten a.m. hit, it was like high school letting out with how many employees practically ran out of the door. I didn't need to duck this time because Brody was one of the first out and I was able to squeeze out between him and two other cars. Following him would be rough until we got back to the mainland from the island the hospital was on. I had to keep those two cars between us so he didn't think he was being followed.

Once we got onto the mainland and onto more crowded streets, I could pace him from a few lanes over. He looked wiped out, but he went right to the gym. As he pulled in, I kept driving. I hit a red and texted Julie that I wouldn't be in today, that I didn't sleep last night. I wasn't quite lying.

I got home, rinsed off, and climbed into bed. Minion jumped up with me, not seeming to care about her breakfast, and curled up in my hair.

I woke to darkness and didn't care. I needed some hydration and food, then I'd go back to sleep and wake back up for another day at the office. Then I glanced at the clock. I wouldn't be going into the office tomorrow—we're closed on Saturdays.

Minion eyed me sleepily and stretched with me before going downstairs for sustenance. It felt nice enough for me to turn the air up, but I knew better. March in Florida had mood swings; some years, it was really nice out, and others, not so much. I wasn't taking chances. A full dinner at midnight wasn't the best idea for me, but I fed Minion and gave her a little extra, which she happily smushed her tiny face into.

I poured a glass of water and grabbed some fruit and yogurt from the fridge. I snacked to the sounds on Minion's crunching and told her, more than once, to slow down or she'd throw up. I know that sounded like some motherly cliché, but she really would puke if she ate too fast. It happened more frequently than I cared to admit.

I finished my food and two glasses of water before going back to bed. Minion came up as I drifted into the blackness of sleep, curling herself back into my hair. *At least we could wake up a little later*, I thought just before sleep set in. Man was I wrong.

Six a.m., and I was wide awake. I stared at the ceiling for what felt like an eternity. In reality, it was only ten minutes. I got up and got myself ready for my daily jog.

Minion, again, stared disapprovingly at me. I petted her as I brushed my teeth and again as I tied my shoes. I jogged down the stairs, stretched, and was gone. It was a cool morning, the sun just barely peeking over the bay. I crossed paths with one of the local meteorologists and waved. He waved back, and we both kept on our way with our earbuds in, mouthing the words to our favorite jogging songs. I jogged farther north than usual and back home. The weather was so beautiful, I almost didn't want to go inside, but I was sweaty and hungry.

Minion was sitting on the stairs silently judging me, her favorite thing to do from her favorite place. I petted her but suddenly stopped. The hairs on my arms and the back of my neck stood up. I crept up the stairs to my nightstand, pulling my Shield EZ from the drawer and flicking the safety off. I swept the second floor. Nothing. I tiptoed back down the stairs, slowly sweeping the house. Someone was in the kitchen, and I pointed the pistol at the back of their head.

"Hands up, and turn around slowly, asshole."

He did as he was told, motioning to pull his hood back. I slid my finger to the trigger, and he put his hands back up. This home invader knew guns and paid attention to small details.

"John, that you?"

"Yes."

I pointed the gun down toward the floor and shot him in the foot.

Ten

He jumped at the sound before he felt the pain—it was deafening in such an enclosed space without ear protection. My ears rang, but I didn't care. I was livid.

He was bleeding from the hole in his foot, all over my kitchen floor. I'm pretty sure it wasn't sanitary, but as long as I got him and the rug he was standing on out of the house fast enough, it might not look like a crime scene. I was also glad I had plenty of peroxide to clean up whatever was left. I shooed him outside, threw out the rug, and picked up the shell casing. He grumbled and groaned as he pulled his phone out of his pocket.

"Why'd you shoot me?"

"Trespasser. I was standing my ground. The real question is what the hell were you doing in my house without an invitation. I don't want to know how you got in, either."

"I thought we could go to brunch after your jog."

"That's the lamest excuse. Admit it: You still think I'm a killer. You were snooping. Well, let me remind you that no one – *fucking no one* – you work with agrees with you. Not your bosses, not your coworkers, not even the fucking janitor!" My voice started to raise, and we were out on the patio. "Deep breath… Okay, what do you really want? Why are you here?"

"I wanted to surprise you." He hung his head like a scolded puppy.

"You're the fucking worst, John. You keep pushing the boundaries—outright crossing some—I set. Now you're bleeding on my patio because I shot you. I shot a cop. Jesus, John! You know I keep loaded guns in the house!"

I couldn't keep my cool; I wanted to shoot him again and again. I walked inside to grab a towel for him to put on the hole in his foot and brought it to him as he spoke to the dispatcher.

"I don't want to hear from or see you. *I* decide if and when we talk again. Got it?" I hadn't been this angry since Alex pulled almost the same thing. I secretly hoped John pressed charges; I'd press them right back. Florida's Stand Your Ground law was wide open and was vaguely written on purpose by the lawyers. Not that it would have mattered. He had made a way into my house, openly trespassed, and got shot. End of story. Who did that? Apparently, the cop I was sleeping with who clearly still thought I was a murderer; that's who.

The ambulance arrived, and I physically pushed him out of my house, blood dripping everywhere as he hopped along. I strung together a whole lot of cuss words in the way only I could and went for the black rags, bucket, peroxide, and water. I grunted and talked angrily to myself as I cleaned the blood off the floor. I really liked that rug, too—it had really tied the room together—and now I had to get a new one because

John had been dumber than Alex. I blew the air out of my lungs so hard it hurt.

Minion stared at me. I hadn't noticed when she came in the kitchen, but I told her not to lick the floor. She walked over to her food bowl and chewed on what was left.

"Wait a second," I said to her, "look at me."

She stopped eating and did.

"You're a terrible attack cat."

She winked at me and went back to her dish.

I huffed, threw away the rags, dumped the bucket in the downstairs bathtub, and went up to take a shower. I let the water burn my skin, but I was still so mad I barely felt it. I needed something else physical to release the anger. I could go for another jog, which would mean another shower, but another shower was nothing in the grand scheme of things.

I turned the water off, dried myself, and changed. Minion wasn't happy at all when I took off out the door again. Neither was I. A police car came rolling up to my house. *Shit.* I didn't want to talk to him; I wanted to jog. I was too pissed off. He got out of the car. He was short, overweight, thinning hair, and red faced, like his blood pressure would be too high for the rest of his life.

"Miss Cage?"

"Yes, Officer?" I walked over to his car so he didn't die in my driveway. I'd already dealt with shooting a cop today; a coronary was the last thing I needed.

"Would you like to press charges against Officer John Sweet for trespassing and breaking and entering?"

"Yes and no. Yes because I want to teach him a lesson. No because he's a good guy and a good cop; he just made a mistake." I stopped and thought about it. "Can I think about it for a day or so?"

"You sure can," he said, handing me his card, "I'm Officer Jones. Here's my card. Call me tomorrow, and let me know. After that, I can't promise the state won't press charges."

"Okay, thanks," I said and jogged off. Officer Jones took the long way out of the neighborhood.

Up Bayshore I jogged again, this time debating if I wanted to send a good cop to jail or, at the absolute least, put him on probation with a restraining order. I wanted to teach him a lesson about crossing boundaries, so I decided to call Officer Jones and let him know I would be pressing charges. It sucked to have to do this, but what choice did I have? I mean, I was pretty sure I'd be losing my almost daily sex, but that wasn't my point. He still thought I was a killer, so he had to go. If he went to prison, even for thirty days, that was my window to kill Brody. It was more than enough time for the stalk, prep, and kill. I'd be fine.

I jogged back home, took another shower, and called Officer Jones after I got dressed. He assured me Sweet would be prosecuted to the fullest extent of the law, particularly because he was a cop and no one liked a dirty cop. I thanked him and hung up. Then I called Julie and asked her to come over so I could tell her all about it and catch up from this week, since I'd barely been in the office. She excitedly agreed.

When she walked through my front door, she was carrying a couple bags and some coffee. I took the coffee holder from her, so she didn't drop it, and set into the kitchen.

She followed.

"I got us both lattes and donuts and bagels and cream cheese."

"Julie, it's almost noon."

"And there's always room for breakfast," she pointedly said as she pulled everything out of the bags.

She had me there. I couldn't disagree. We sat and drank our coffee, Julie filling me in on the details of the week, when my phone rang. The display showed Unknown. I answered it.

"Brit, it's John—"

He used his one phone call to call me. "For a smart guy, you really are *fucking* stupid," I said before hanging up.

Eleven

"HE REALLY JUST CALLED you?" Julie asked. We both had looks of disgust on our faces.

I was wondering what he could possibly say to me to make things any better. Don't get me wrong, I wasn't 100 percent sold on the restraining order, but at the same time it would allow me room to work. None of his bosses or coworkers who knew me thought I was a killer; they thought he was crazy.

Maybe I would go through with the restraining order. Would he have someone else follow me? Doubtful. I'd realize if someone was, but I knew they wouldn't. They'd prefer to be at a coffee shop hanging out than to follow the girl Sweet used to bang for the sole purpose of keeping tabs on her because he thought she was a killer when no one else did.

"I don't know what made him think I'd want to talk to him. He couldn't even look me in the eye when I asked him if he still thought I was Alex's killer."

Julie's face turned white. "Really?" She couldn't believe I was a killer any more than she could believe I was still sleeping with him after he wouldn't admit he still thought I was. It was all so convoluted and stupid. Yes, I was a killer, but no one actually *knew*. The only person who suspected anything was now behind bars and wouldn't be allowed near me in less than twenty-four hours. It was almost like I'd never started sleeping with him in the first place. Almost.

He'd still do what he could to get back in my good graces. Not that I'd let him back in, but I had to keep him close enough to know what he was up to where I was concerned. I hated the idea of making him beg for my forgiveness, but I resigned that it might be necessary.

I grabbed a bagel and put a hefty amount of cream cheese on it before closing it like a sandwich and taking a huge bite. It was so unhealthy but tasted so good. It was a poppy bagel, too, which was one of my favorites. Julie knew me well and was too good to me. She said the same about me, though, so I guess we were even. We ate in silence, sipping our coffee.

I broke the silence, asking if Julie had any thoughts on my delay of opening a second office. She did and agreed. It had taken me long enough to find her, and while we were growing, it wasn't at so rapid a pace that the new office was needed yet. I knew I'd need to find a Julie 2.0 who could run the branch, and my search wouldn't be easy, even with all my contacts and feelers.

She did mention that she would be comfortable running either office; she'd gotten used to it while I was out most of the week. I knew she would be fine if left to her own devices. I hoped it made her more confident in her abilities, but asking her would only make her shy away. That's just the kind of person she was. I'd be patient and wait for her to tell me when she felt she was ready.

We finished out coffees and bagels and cleaned up the kitchen table.

Julie hugged me and left, having made plans with Cody for the afternoon. I decided to veg out on the couch with Minion and watch mindless rom-coms, comedies, horror, and whatever else I felt like. I fell asleep at some point, and the ringing of my phone woke me up. Another Unknown. I wasn't answering it this time. Whoever it was could leave a message. Then I went into the settings and set the function that blocks unknown callers and sends them straight to voice mail. I never turned it on in the first place because of work, but now that John was locked up, I wasn't playing games with anyone. If the call was that important…

The next time I woke up, it was after nine. I fed Minion and went up to bed. I wasn't hungry and just wanted my bed. I felt wiped out—mentally, emotionally, and physically—and I hadn't the slightest clue why. All I could think was all the drama with John and the subsequent abuse of my body with a second jog.

The physical abuse was fine, though. I preferred to get negative energy out that way. And it sure wasn't the first time I'd jogged more than once in one day. I remember before I killed Alex I jogged twice in a day and didn't feel as bad as I did. Did I actually care about John? Maybe I did somewhere deep down, and I was in some kind of denial about it. The last time my emotions kicked my ass was when Osten had his heart attack.

I lay down and closed my eyes. I was so beat, I didn't even feel Minion curl up in my hair. Tomorrow might be Monday, but I had appearances to keep so no one suspected anything. I'd be at the gym at the usual time then follow Brody from there. Maybe tomorrow would be the day I figured out the kill spot.

I woke knowing I still had the abandoned garage in Ybor, but I didn't want to risk using that twice in a row. Maybe twice in five kills or something, but not for this one. Maybe I'd look for something near the dump site. I wouldn't have to travel so far with a dead body in my Jeep, like I did with Alex in his car before I had it crushed.

I figured I'd leave Brody's truck out in a mudhole somewhere. This way, when he came up missing, the cops would think he got stuck in the hole somehow. Those were out in Pasco County, and my Jeep would fit in among the rest of the vehicles. I just needed to plan the swap. It was forming in my head as I got ready for my day.

I'd drop my Jeep at the mud spot least populated and do like I did with Alex's Honda, only leave Brody's truck there. People knew he went mudding, so it wouldn't be anything unusual for his truck to be there. When he didn't come back, there would be no body, no evidence. Just his truck covered in mud. His body would have long been devoured by pigs.

A smirk spread across my face as I got dressed thinking about it. I'd long ago researched how long it took pigs to eat humans, and I had the perfect place to try it out for real. Granted, I didn't have my own Sardinian pigs; there was a local livestock farm, complete with dozens of swine. I finished getting ready, fed Minion, and left for the office.

Twelve

OFFICER JONES CALLED THE office to make sure I was okay and to assure me that if I wanted to talk to a victim's advocate, he could put me in touch with one. I informed him I was fine and asked the status of John's arraignment. He said John was remanded to custody and sent to solitary, given how inmates react to cops in general population. He told me the restraining order had also gone through but that John probably wouldn't be released for two years or more, unless he got off early for good behavior. It was unlikely because he was a cop and knew the laws. And I was fully within mine to shoot him. I'd already called my lawyer in case I needed to show in court, but he spoke to the judge and played the PTSD card. I'd never see John Sweet again until he was released from whichever Florida state prison he'd be sent to. I thanked Officer Jones for calling to inform me and hung up.

Julie overheard the whole conversation and came in to chat about it. She, too, kept making sure I was okay. I reassured her I was fine and not traumatized. I was fine sleeping at night and not afraid to go home, though I did start carrying my Glock when I went anywhere. Unless I went for a jog; then the Shield went with me for practical reasons—it was a compact gun, so I could carry it easier.

"Brit, will you take me shooting?"

"What? Why? You don't need a gun, Julie."

"I just want to know what it feels like."

"That's it? I don't know…maybe. I'll think about it."

Julie looked a little defeated but understood my hesitation. She'd never held a gun before; she had no need for one. I had problems in the past that made me cautious; I kept just the two, but guns were a lot like tattoos—you always wanted more.

Julie had gone back to her desk, and I looked up Brody's address on a map. I'd gotten it from my friend at the gym; now it was recon time. Using satellite view, I looked at his place from every aerial direction, then from the street. It didn't look like much. Then again, I didn't expect much from him; he didn't come off at particularly smart. I swore he was one of those dumb jocks that only graduated because he was on the football team. But that didn't explain his nursing degree. I was sure he'd paid someone off for that. There was no way he knew which organ was which.

With his house scoped as much as I could from a map, I wrote the address on a sticky note folded in half and put it in my purse. I'd have to check the place out at night, with or without him there. Preferably with him there so I could learn his patterns.

I would just follow him home from the gym tonight. I needed to know all of his patterns, starting with what he did post-workout. I didn't care if all he did was shower and go to sleep. To properly kill someone, one must know the prey's patterns and lifestyle. I mean the cannibal doctor knew most of his prey on a very personal level. I didn't want to know those I killed like that—I had a long time ago, and I still occasionally felt pangs of regret for one of them. Cassie was a good girl…

I let the day pass by with approvals and supply orders and interviews I merely watched from what felt like someone else's eyes. Julie was good at this. I was selfish for wanting to keep her to myself, but we'd also determined this office wasn't busy enough to warrant the renting of another. Yet.

We'd get there, and if Osten and the rest of my clients had anything to say about it, it would be sooner than later. They were all growing at a substantial pace and were trying to push me along with them, but I simply wasn't there yet. I would be in the next six months or so, but I wasn't rushing anything, either.

We left and hugged bye, Julie saying something about getting together for dinner soon. I agreed but wasn't sure how much I meant it. Did I want to be around such a lovey couple? I really had to think about it. Jules and Cody were the best couple I knew. They fit together like chicken and Alfredo; they were so cute it was nauseating.

I'd decided that if and when I got into a real relationship, something like theirs would be what I wanted. Maybe not all the cutesy shit, but the romance and love and intimacy. If it did happen, I wanted someone I wouldn't grow bored of, someone I'd always be sexually attracted to. But was any of that even real?

It was chilly, so I turned the heat on in my Jeep on the way home. I went in, fed Minion, and changed into warm, comfy pajamas and started a fire. I pulled my tablet out of my bag and started mapping out possible routes between the gym and Brody's house and the hospital. The routes were challenging, mainly due to heavy traffic, depending on time of day. I needed to go to the gym tonight to start figuring out his patterns. I still didn't know if he showered at the gym or hospital, if he stopped for food between… Things like that made all the difference. It was close to seven by the time I decided I needed to go tonight, so I changed and left.

I worked out like nothing was wrong. A few people stopped and asked about John, and I had to explain he was locked up for trespassing and that he basically broke into my house. I felt pretty bad saying it, but I wasn't about to lie to anyone. What he'd done was inexcusable and unforgivable. I'd eventually *act* like I forgave him, but that day was far away. Like the saying goes, "Keep your friends close and your enemies closer." And I can promise you John was no friend. At least, with him out of the way, I had no one to interfere or cause trouble with my killer life.

Brody and his lunkhead buddies went into the locker room and were there for quite some time. Brody shaved his head so there really wasn't a foolproof way for me to tell if he'd showered or not, but he did have his scrubs on, as I suspected he would. I knew he had work tonight.

His wearing the scrubs made me believe he did take a shower here. One less thing to worry about. I ducked out the door before anyone could notice and hopped into my Jeep, starting it and making it look like I was busy fiddling with the radio as Brody walked to his truck. He got in and pulled out of the lot. I followed, staying a few cars back so he didn't notice the tail. He got onto 275 South, and so did I. I was so into paying attention to him, I almost sideswiped a Durango with tinted windows. When I'd gotten my bearings back, I couldn't find Brody's truck.

Thirteen

I SPED UP AND found him two miles south, so I backed off a bit.

He was in the far-left lane, and I had a difficult time keeping up with him. He was going at least ninety, and I may have on occasion beat on my Jeep, but I wasn't about to push her like that, let alone risk him seeing that he was being followed.

He finally got into the right lane to get off at the exit for the hospital. I followed and didn't park until he did, slowly circling until he walked inside. Then I backed in and settled down for the remainder of his shift. Maybe he'd fight with someone else, or even the same person, again tonight. Dude clearly has an anger issue, which I planned to use to my advantage. An argument gone wrong lead to his disappearance. The cops would pull his phone records, find out he'd been yelling at someone and threatening them…

The grab and kill spots still eluded me, irritating me to no immediate end. I dredged the recesses of my twisted mind and still had issues coming up with something. Maybe I'd use an idea from a movie or TV show. It was sad I couldn't think of my own way to get this handled. I was a disappointment to the club of serial killers everywhere. Actually, I was just a disappointment to myself.

In reality, not very many serial killers were original in their methods. BTK, Dahmer, Holmes…Gein. They were original. Hell, Gein was inspiration for multiple fictional serial killers who wore people's skin. Don't get me wrong: I'd thought about it once or twice, but that was the kind of thing that required an immense amount of patience, and I wasn't sure I had it in me. Sure, I could keep the skin supple and clean enough to attempt wearing it, but the stalk and the kill would have to be so precisely executed, I really didn't believe I had the kind of time or patience it would need.

This was how I passed the time while I waited. Thinking about future kills instead of properly figuring this one out. Dammit. I punched the steering wheel, accidentally hitting the horn. I frantically looked around but saw no one. I let out a sigh of relief.

I had yet to look inside Brody's house; that was next on my list. Maybe I'd find some inspiration there. If I couldn't, then I'd really have a problem. I didn't mean using his house as a kill site, either. But maybe there was something inside, like a photo of him as a kid somewhere or an implement I wouldn't have to "borrow" from the gym. Maybe he had dumbbells at home. A girl could hope with a muscle-bound douche like him. He was definitely the type to have a home gym. I'd have to go when he was on a day shift. I had his schedule at home and would check it when I got back.

The night was a bore and, essentially, a bust. Nothing happened, and I had to stop myself from falling asleep a few times. Finally, the sun rose—right in my eyes—keeping me awake and blinded. I thanked nature for the assist. A few hours later, Brody walked out, seeming in a good mood. I followed him home and went back to my house. I called Julie, telling her Minion was puking and I wanted to keep an eye on her. It was the lamest excuse I'd used in quite some time for not going in. Disappointment again. Not that I was disappointing anyone but myself; it was the principle of the matter.

I looked over the notes I had on Brody's schedule before going to sleep. He worked day shift on Saturday. That would be when I went into his house and got the layout. I was glad his neighbors seemed like they were rarely home. I don't remember if I even took my sneakers off before I flopped onto my bed and passed out.

The sun painted a beautiful picture as it set when I woke. Minion was on my chest, drooling on my neck. I laughed and petted her. My watch read seven thirty, and I picked Minion up so I could sit up. I blinked and rubbed my eyes. Minion rubbed hers.

I ran a hand over my face, thinking about the day and the days before and the days leading up to killing Brody. I really needed a cleanable place or someplace out of the way where no one would notice blood. Why was my brain not operating properly? It frustrated the hell out of me. I stood and walked into the kitchen, calling Minion as I did so I could feed her. Then I went to my room and started flipping through movies and TV shows on Netflix and Prime. I *would* figure something out, even if I really did steal it from fiction.

I hit play on some cheesy B movie. The next thing I knew, my alarm was blaring. Fuck me. I got dressed for my jog, hoping it would clear my head, even if only a little. I needed some kind of idea, but when I tried, I fell asleep. Was I exhausted? Did I need to go to the doctor, or was I just wearing myself out with the overnights watching Brody? That was probably the issue. I was so used to going to sleep by midnight and waking up at six that being up all night felt like something I was too old to do anymore. If I wanted, I could probably keep it up, but I really didn't want to.

My brain and body weren't too happy with me for the duration of my jog, either. I was an uncoordinated mess, and though I never really cared about time—just distance—it took entirely too long. What normally took me twenty minutes took almost double. My brain screamed at me, and my body was as limp as a soggy noodle.

Minion screamed at me, too, when I got back; she wanted breakfast. I fed her, took a shower, dried off, and just sat on my bed. I had to go in today. If I didn't, Julie would definitely think something was wrong. The only thing wrong was my lack of sleep. I stood and picked out something more casual than what I usually wore and put more makeup on than normal to cover the dark circles under my eyes. Today was going to be a long day.

Fourteen

WHEN I SAID EARLIER that today was going to be long, that was an understatement. Holy hell, it was a never-ending Thursday. I'd had slow days before, but this one was the slowest ever. For now, anyway.

I kept my office door closed all day after telling Julie I wasn't feeling well. Of course, she told me I should've stayed home. I brushed her off, saying something about I had approvals or something. I had to try to find some kind of floor plan or layout of Brody's house online, so I went to every real estate site I could find until I found one with photos from before he bought it. There wasn't much about the layout he could change; I was grateful for the knowledge imparted on me by my father about load-bearing walls and such.

If the back door was still the same, it was a painfully easy lock to pick. I had a kit, but I also had a snap gun to use when necessary. One way or another, I was getting inside that house on Saturday. I just needed to survive today and tomorrow. I knew I was going to crash hard tonight and that I couldn't skip the gym. Brody and his friends were stupid, but they might suspect something, so I had to keep up appearances. Sometimes there was nothing I despised more than that. Faking nice was one thing; faking nice to assholes like them was something altogether different.

The day was finally over, and I went home, changed, and ran to the gym. I told myself I'd do a minimal machine work and get out. Then I ran into four people I hadn't seen in months, and they all wanted to catch up. These people were friends, so I didn't want to be rude. I told two of them to call me and we'd make dinner plans and the other two, not that we were ever that close, I talked with for a few minutes before ducking out.

I made sure Brody and his cretin friends saw me. Then I jumped into my Jeep and floored it out of there. All I wanted to do was sleep. Rush hour was just starting to end; then again, south Tampa was a hotspot for traffic at all times. It was hellish.

When I finally backed into my driveway, Officer Jones was waiting for me. *Now what?*

"Hey, Jones! What can I do for you?" I asked as I jumped down and locked and armed the Jeep.

He exited his cruiser. "I just wanted to make sure he was leaving you alone. I heard he called you before the restraining order went through, and I, well, I'm really sorry he acted that way." He looked at his feet, his face flushing in embarrassment.

I put a hand on his shoulder. "It's okay. I'm okay. Thanks for stopping by. I really appreciate it. But you know you don't have to worry about me. And don't be sorry for his actions. They were his and his alone. Don't make excuses for him."

Jones lifted his head and smiled at me. "Thanks, Brit. If I can call you that? Honestly, none of us even knows where he got it in his head that you're a killer." He shook his head.

"It's okay, really. And yes, please call me Brit. Now, if you'll excuse me, I'm fresh from the gym and desperately need a shower and sleep."

He stepped back. "Sorry to bother you. Like I said, I wanted to make sure you were all right. If you need anything…"

"I'll be sure to call you. Good night." I waved and unlocked my front door. I didn't move once I'd closed and locked it behind me until I knew Jones was gone.

Looked like I had a straggler who would most likely patrol the neighborhood now, just to ensure my safety. His crush was cute, but he sure as shit wasn't the type I'd even consider sleeping with. He'd do for information, though.

I fed Minion, showered, and went to bed. I didn't care that it was only around eight thirty when my head hit the pillow. I cared that I needed sleep. The house was dark and peaceful. I set my white noise app and drifted into the most peaceful sleep I'd had since killing Alex.

Tossing and turning, sweating… Minion bit me, and I felt the wet, hot blood roll down my arm. I bolted upright. My eyes were wide open. I'd been scared awake by a nightmare that not only got me but Minion, too.

My hand looked worse than it was, but I got out of bed, dressed the wound, and changed the sheets. I stopped for a glass of water after setting the sheets to soak in water with some peroxide mixed in. I chugged the glass then drained the washer and set it to wash.

I knew I wasn't going back to sleep anytime soon, so I sat on the couch and watched mindless sitcoms until the washer stopped and I could make sure all the blood came out and could dry the sheets. All was well, so into the dryer they went. I sat back on the couch, trying to recall any bits from that dream that scared even my cat.

Brody had wrapped his hands around my neck, and I had used some move I saw in a movie once to break the hold and stabbed him in the eye, then slit his throat, blood spraying everywhere. Severed arteries did that. I was covered in his blood in his house. I slipped on the floor and fell. Somehow, I'd been wearing all white; now it was dark red and dripping. I tried to get up but kept sliding. Finally, I grabbed a doorway to help steady me and slipped my way back to an awkward standing position. I was standing on a slip and slide of blood and vinyl flooring. I slipped again, losing my grip on the doorframe, and banged my head on the way down…

The recollection made me unnecessarily angry. If it hadn't been almost sunrise, I'd have gone for a jog to rid myself of the negative energy I still felt, even after watching the sitcoms.

I grabbed one of the decorative pillows off the couch next to me and tore it wide open. This wasn't good; it had been years since I was this angry over something so small. It was a nightmare, not a premonition.

I needed to go back to sleep. I turned the TV off, grabbed an ice pack from the freezer, and went back to bed, ice pack on my eyes so maybe I wouldn't need so much concealer in a few hours.

Fifteen

THE ICE PACK WAS warm and made a sick sloshing thump when it hit the floor as I rolled over. Minion jumped and looked around, trying to figure out what the noise was. Her fur was standing at all kinds of weird angles. I chuckled and petted her, letting her know it was nothing to worry about. She purred in my face, nuzzling my nose, as I pulled the blankets off me and stretching.

I picked the ice pack up off the floor and threw it on the bed before going to the closet to pick out the day's outfit and shower. Minion expressed her disapproval in her usual pathetic tones. I petted her head and went about my morning ritual.

When I got out of the shower, I checked my eyes in the mirror. They looked much better, but I'd need tea bags or a spa day to make the circles go away fully. No big deal; that's what Sunday was for. Tomorrow, however, was for sneaking around someone's house while they worked.

I pulled my mind back to today and the concealer I needed to wear. The majority of my stalk came at night, so why was I so irritated by how awful my puffy eyes looked? I didn't know, but I probably needed to run it by

Ben at some point and figure it out. My phone chirped from a text message. I put the concealer down and went to check the phone. It was Julie. She was running late.

"No worries. Hope all is okay," I sent back and went back to the concealer. Makeup finished, I grabbed my phone and went down to feed Minion, put shoes on, and grab my bag.

I walked outside and couldn't breathe. July in Tampa was awful and would be followed by a further extended inability to breathe fresh air, otherwise known as August, the month where everyone swore the state moved closer to the sun. It never mattered how many showers I took or how many changes of clothes—I'd sweat through it all.

I had a shower in my bathroom at the office that I rarely used. Other than that, it collected dust, and the cleaning people cleaned it. I'd have been lying if I said I didn't have thoughts all the way to work about taking a shower or two before I went home today.

I parked in the lot, and it seemed like every other office had closed for a beach day. We did those things, but summers were traditionally busy for us, largely because of college kids looking for summer jobs. I unlocked the door and went in.

Not even ten minutes later, there was one of the aforementioned college students in the reception area. I had to laugh to myself before greeting them. It was a previous employee who missed working for me and wanted to come back. I asked if she wanted to come back through the semester also, and she gave an enthusiastic reply. I had a reputation for getting employees higher pay and better jobs, so her excitement wasn't unwarranted. We shook hands, I told her I'd be in touch, and she went on her way. I loved killing people, but it sure felt good to help a few of them, too, now and again.

Julie came in around eleven, apologizing profusely and muttering something about a doctor appointment. My face lit up as I asked her to come into my office to tell me about it. Of course, I held my cool—despite her not letting me know beforehand that she hadn't let me know beforehand—and played the *Is everything okay?* card.

Naturally, all was well. She thought she was pregnant and had been really excited, but it turned out she was just late. She excitedly told me that she and Cody wanted a family, but she wasn't sold on the idea unless they were married—largely because of finances and the inevitably sky-high cost of insuring a newborn. I told her not to worry. I also told her not to rely on a man for anything. She understood, especially after what had happened with Sweet when we weren't even officially together. I imagined that if we had been together, I would've killed him instead of shot him. Hell, I'd probably even had admitted to it.

Julie also filled me in on what else was going on in her life, considering I hadn't been around much. She and Cody were shopping around for a house to buy. They had even tried to buy the one they were living in, but the owner shot them down.

She was smart and called one of the realtors we worked with to aid in the search and one of the local bankers about mortgage approval. That part hinged on her, since Cody made little cash and most of that in tips. And who claimed all of their tips? Cody was graduating this fall, too, which meant he likely didn't have as much credit history as Julie.

I was so happy for Julie's happiness, I forgot about my own issues for the day. I almost forgot what this felt like. I promised her I'd try to be in the office more and that I had some personal things going on, but I was healthy, just on some kind of anxiety tear or something. It would pass, but I'd need extra meetings with Ben and possible medication. It happened more frequently than I cared to admit, but Julie knew; she sensed it.

Julie hugged me and went back to her desk and I back to plotting how best not to be seen getting into Brody's house. There was a wooded area behind the house and a door close enough to those woods. It was on the rear corner where the carport for that obnoxious truck met the house. If I snuck from the woods, I should be able to pop in unnoticed. The last time I was in his neighborhood, it seemed like most of his neighbors were snowbirds, with newspapers piled up in the driveways and no one to be seen. Not even a stray cat, which was odd. Then again, we also had coyotes here and there, so it wasn't entirely impossible any strays had been a meal. I hated that thought. That's part of why Minion was never allowed out of the house except onto the screened-in patio. I had a harness and leash for her, too, and sometimes we'd go for walks, but the ground would burn her tiny beans right now. Maybe in December we could walk again. Maybe I'd even see if she'd jog with me. Yes, she was weird. She was my cat.

I mapped out Brody's address again, satellite view and street, and mentally ran through tomorrow's plans. I seemed easy enough, but I couldn't shake the nightmare. Was it telling me to wait because he might be home? If he were home, I'd keep driving and plan another day to get the layout.

His house was ideal to kidnap him from and transport him using his own truck, and it was looking more like my possible kill spot. The kill spot was the only issue I'd faced. I'd figure that out and move on. Maybe I'd kill him at the mudhole where I was going to leave his truck. That was a really bad idea, though, because the cops would look for signs of foul play in and around the truck. I needed a separate place for the kill, like I did with Alex, and another for the body dump. I already had the rest of the pieces of the puzzle: rubber gloves, contractor bags, bucket, peroxide…and if Brody had a home gym, that would likely be where and how I killed him. A repeat of Alex's body transport sounded more plausible now. A smile spread slowly across my face lips. Some of my anxiety began to thaw.

Sixteen

SATURDAY CAME FASTER THAN anticipated. I went for my jog and didn't bother to shower after; I figured I'd smell better than the inside of Brody's house.

I did a quick drive-by to make sure his truck wasn't there and parked in the woods behind his house. That alone made me love my Jeep even more. I crept through to the back corner, where the house and carport met, looking and listening to everything around me. I heard a dog bark in the distance but nothing close enough to make me think anyone was inside.

I picked the lock too easily—it was only the doorknob. He sure felt comfortable in this neighborhood. Hadn't even installed a deadbolt.

I found myself standing in a utility room that stank like sweaty jockstraps and almost threw up. I covered my nose and mouth and tiptoed my way through the only other doorway. It led to a short hallway. There were no other doors in the hallway; it ended at the living room.

Here is where I stood, mouth gaping, in surprise. Brody had good taste. A glass coffee table, light gray sofa-and-love-seat set, black entertainment center with the sixty-inch TV hanging in the center. The room looked like an ad right from the Ikea catalog. The floor was gray wood laminate, the kind I had at home and adored. He had family photos and high school photos hanging, along with his nursing degree. He was a happy and proud man. Shame he was a shitty human at the gym and to most women he encountered there. Typical, I supposed, but gross nonetheless. I wasn't sure I had much of a plan for looking at the rest of the house, so I let my senses guide me. Next was the kitchen.

I was blown away by its simplicity and the beauty that it held within. Soft-close drawers, a center island with dishwasher and sink, flat-top stove, built-in wall microwave and oven. I could live in this kitchen and always find new beauty in it. I was impressed and offended. How could he have such good taste yet be so disgusting? It really was mind-boggling. I managed to behave myself and not touch anything, not even the stainless appliances—something told me they were the ones that resisted fingerprints, but I wasn't about to find out for sure. There was a dining room off the side of the kitchen that held a black wooden table and matching chairs. A solitary window was in the opposite wall from the doorway.

I wandered out of the dining room, back through the kitchen, and into one of three bedrooms and two bathrooms. This must have been the in-law suite, as it sat a little farther back than the other bedrooms and was decorated in more of an older person's style. Flowered wallpaper, light pinks and greens… I shivered. The room was dusty, and I felt a sneeze coming on, so I ducked out quickly to not disturb the dust.

The next doorway led to a guest room. Another grayish tone with white trim and the same laminate floor, with a white area rug under the queen-size bed. There was no bathroom in this room, but it did have a decent-size closet.

Continuing my walk led to the master bedroom and bath. Complete with walk-in closet and a glass sliding door that I assumed led to a deck of sorts. It was confirmed when I walked over to peer through the door. This room, like the rest, had the laminate, gray walls, white baseboards, and crown molding, with a king-size bed on a white area rug. Before poking through the bathroom, I decided to try the closet, immediately regretting it. The stench was worse than the utility room. I backed out, closing the door and bolting to the bathroom. I leaned over the toilet and prayed to the porcelain goddess. Thankfully, it was clean.

The man kept a clean home, even if certain rooms smelled something close to death. It was tastefully decorated, minus the dead-mother-obsession room.

I heard something outside and looked out the bathroom window. Just a car driving by. Whew! That could've been bad.

I poked around a little more, not finding much else of interest in the bathroom. On my way back to the living room, I noticed a small room just barely noticeable unless you looked dead at it. I poked my head in. It was a weight room, complete with free weights and a bench with barbells. I knew this would be here. Even better for me was the vinyl flooring. I could lay out a few cut-open contractor bags and do my work. This really couldn't have been any more perfect.

I ducked back out through the nasty utility room, locking the door behind me. I jogged back to my Jeep and carefully drove out of the neighborhood. Could this have been more predictable? There wasn't much to think about on the ride home except when I was going to do this. I knew I had to wait a long enough period of time for everyone to forget Brody and I had words. Maybe three more weeks or so.

The waiting, as usual, was going to suck. I hated waiting, and every time I was forced to in one way or another, I heard "Waiting on a Friend" by The Rolling Stones. It was like a curse, but the song spoke so much truth. If it was worth it, it would be worth the wait. At least that's what I was told growing up. In my experiences, however, sometimes it was, and others it wasn't. Mostly it was. Take Sweet; he was the perfect example.

I bided my time, and lo and behold, he acted like a fool, broke into my house, got shot *and* fired. I'd call that a win in any playbook.

Seventeen

THE WAITING GAME STARTED pretty much the moment I left Brody's house. And it went on and on. Two days would feel like two months, and continue feeling that way until I could finally kill that fucker. I couldn't believe it was only Monday and I was already ready to go. That wasn't a good sign, though. If I was ready to move now, it meant I was missing something supply-wise. This had happened a few times before when I couldn't wait, and I missed a few trash bags and some duct tape. Those weren't exactly small "oopses" either. Forgetting duct tape was the equivalent of having to sign a contract with no pens anywhere.

My kill bag was still in the safe where I kept it. I pulled it out each night and went through it, silently taking note of what was there. I hoped I'd pick up on what was missing if I kept going through it. I didn't want to write a list out—I avoided that at all costs. Or I thought I could, anyway.

I had started a mental list of what I had in the bag: contractor bags, rubber gloves, various knives, zip ties, peroxide. I determined I needed another bottle of peroxide, another bucket, since I'd burned the one I used when I killed Alex, and maybe more chains. Not that I had a clue what I'd bolt the chains to for keeping Brody immobile. Maybe I could drug him somehow?

I stopped and thought about if I knew any veterinarians who worked with horses—or any veterinarians, really. Ketamine was a powerful drug, but I also knew they'd do a toxicology when they found the body. I hoped it wouldn't be for weeks, but Brody would be dead, with no metabolism or any other bodily functions to work the drug out of his system. I'd need about three cc's of ketamine, which meant I'd have a whole lot of extra syringes on my hands. Unless… Did I have a diabetic friend I could snag one or two from?

Then came the matter of getting the ketamine. I supposed I could take Minion for her shots and maybe steal a bottle or two from the vet, but I really liked him and didn't want him to know what I needed it for; otherwise, I'd just ask him for the script. He was good like that.

It hit me that psychiatrists could prescribe ketamine, too. So could damn near any doctor. I needed to think long and hard about getting Osten to sign a blank script and me writing out the injectable. If someone happened to find out, though, I didn't want Osten to get in trouble. I needed another doctor. One who couldn't be connected with me in any way. I had military friends who could get their hands on it considering they were nurses and such. That would have to be the way. I learned a long time ago that a lot of things "went missing," particularly in the military. They had a habit of terrible recordkeeping in some units, and their bosses somehow never knew. I'd grab a few burner phones and handle this without either of us getting into trouble.

To recap for myself, I needed one or two vials of ketamine, a few three-cc or higher syringes, more chain, and some way to bolt the chains to the studs in the wall or something. It would probably be the floor. Shit, I needed a way to carry him to my Jeep, too. An engine hoist wasn't practical, and I couldn't carry 360, but I could bench it if challenged. Shit, shit, shit. Maybe a wheelchair would work. Since his head would be broken and covered in blood, I'd already planned to duct-tape the bags around his head like I did with Alex. I didn't want brains leaking in my Jeep, thanks. I could easily get one of those into the backseat area, and Brody would be smushed into the "cargo" area that Jeeps don't really have. Throwing him from the back to the pen would be easy enough; I'd have more leverage than I'd need.

I was exhausted from the day and then the mini meltdown I just had. Minion sat on the bed staring at me.

"What do you want?"

She came over, looked pitiful, and nudged my hand. I petted her for a long time then took her downstairs to feed her and myself. I even gave her a few small pieces of my chicken before I put it in my salad and added the caesar dressing to it. I sat at the table and Minion her bowl. We were both content.

Monday, I'd use a mailing service to mail the burner to my friend over at Fort Hood. He'd get me what I needed and within the required time frame. This felt easier than it would be. I knew the biggest issue I was going to have was Brody's size. He was easily twice mine, and the weight room was at the other end of the damned house. I'd have to leave him in the wheelchair in the utility room while I made sure the weight room was free of blood and brains and anything else; I made a mental note to add two more bottles of peroxide to my kill bag. That should be enough. I knew there would be a lot of blood; I've seen movies and I've seen it in real life.

Brody would be my biggest challenge yet, but I didn't care. He needed to go, and what I had planned was so poetic and perfect. A nasty gym rat whose death was going to be immaculate. The dump site was muddy and gross, sure, but the animals that would dispose of his body were so much cleaner than that. Pigs got such a bad rap. After all, there were pigs, and then there were pigs.

Eighteen

Sunday consisted of food shopping and picking up two burner phones. By food shopping, I mean I ordered and it was delivered, which was still accurate, technically. I knew better than to venture into a Florida grocery store on a Sunday. They were pure insanity; I was a serial killer, not a crazy person.

Not long after I got back home after picking up the phones, the groceries showed up. I tipped the driver and took the bags into the kitchen, Minion on my heels. She enjoyed being in the way of a lot of things, like a typical cat. She jumped on the counter and stuck her little head in bag after bag, sniffing to see if there was anything she wanted. I petted her, picked her up, and set her down on the floor. She screamed at me and walked away. I laughed as I went back to putting food away.

With my control issues, I had a problem with ordering my groceries online, having someone else pick and pack them. I always talked to myself, out loud, as I unpacked the bags about how poorly someone's bagging skills were. Then I told myself that this was my punishment for waiting until Sunday. I had plenty of other days to go; I could stop on my way home on a Tuesday just as easily. Plus, I could use my reusable bags instead of dealing with these awful plastic ones. To recycle them, I had to take them to the store anyway, so how was shopping from home making this any easier for me? If that was my toughest decision all week, I'd be happy, but I knew better. I still had to wait to kill that dumbass Chad of all Chads.

It wouldn't be much longer, but it definitely felt longer. Plus, the time would allow me to get the ketamine and syringes and fully prep. I figured I'd restock all my supplies. The bucket and chain were starting to feel like habit, too, so I decided to grab another of each of them. In all, I exceeded my list by double, but it wasn't like it was all going to sit forever. I killed once every few months to keep the cops guessing. At this rate, I'd be restocking every time I killed, depending on the kill—whether it would be exceptionally messy—and all would be well. I kept everything in the safe except the chains and buckets. I drive a Jeep, so there was a perfect reason to have the chains, especially because I didn't have a winch yet. That was on my list of things to eventually add to it.

I had a whole list of parts I wanted to add for climbing and eventual mudding. I mean, yeah, I did mud every now and then, but it was that serious mudding out in Bartow or wherever—"the sticks," as the old-timers called the rural areas down here. That's also where I planned to leave Brody's truck.

He went mudding as often as he could, so for his truck to be out there wouldn't be anything weird. Maybe weird would strike when someone realized it had been there for days or weeks, but that wasn't my problem. I wouldn't even be the last person seen with him, so there was no way, aside from the argument, Sweet could think I killed him.

Yes, I knew he was in jail, but if he talked enough, someone might actually believe him or agree to follow me for no other reason than to rule me out. I read a book—and watched the coinciding TV show—where a serial killer worked in the police department and another cop suspected him of being a killer and followed him for months. Fiction or not, the killer was almost caught multiple times. In the TV show, anyway. He didn't in the books, but the books were better. People were killed when they should've been, and some were killed in the show who lived in the books. I loved the divergence.

But I tolerated no such divergence in my private killing life. Once I hunted you, only a miracle could keep you from my blade—and I didn't believe in miracles.

I finished putting the groceries away and threw the bags into another bag. *How meta*. I went outside and put all the plastic bags in the back of the Jeep in an effort to remind myself to stop and drop them for proper recycling. When I went back in, I grabbed my laptop and sat at the table, looking up the random mudholes along the back roads that frequently took me to Orlando. I avoided the I-4 because the typically drunk, drugged Florida drivers were way deadlier than I was.

I liked my life and preferred the scenic route, anyway. The most dangerous thing I'd encountered so far on the back-county roads was almost colliding with a quadder who wasn't paying attention. Other than that, there were plenty of safe little mud spots to plant my meathead; I just needed one. I chose one closer to the middle; it was in Pasco County only because the road curved up so high before going back down into neighboring ones. Besides, I needed Pasco County because that's where the livestock farm was. Like I said, it was out in the sticks.

Thinking about that place made me realize I needed to get my ass up there, too. Not only did I need to scope the layout, but I wanted to pet the goats and maybe find out about having one as a pet. I think my only issue would be Minion trying to bite it. Maybe a pygmy goat and she could cuddle with it or something.

There I went again with the crazy ideas. My homeowner's association would never allow something like that. Even if I litter-trained it, some nosy jerk would find out, and that would be the end of that. Not that I'd mind selling this place to go elsewhere, but I was in a pretty convenient location, and that alone was hard to find in Tampa.

I checked the time and looked up the livestock farm. They were open another two hours. I grabbed my things and drove up there.

Nineteen

For a Sunday, there wasn't much traffic headed north. Then again, there really wasn't much any other day, either. Not much happened in Pasco County apart from the meth cooking, the weed growing, and the sex trafficking, and the local sheriff was all in on that shit. I drove five over the speed limit, making great time.

I arrived at the livestock farm in about thirty minutes. There wasn't really a parking lot, more of an empty piece of land, devoid of grass and weeds, all sand. I parked and got out, excited to see the place. Okay, I was excited over seeing lots of goats. I loved goats, in case I hadn't mentioned it before. They were so much fun, regardless that they pooped wherever they want. Literally, they just walked and drop poop pellets everywhere. I guess I could have one of those robotic vacuums follow it around, but again, the damned HOA. Maybe I needed a house in Pasco; they had more land.

I walked over to the pig pen, mentally counting how many grown pigs they had. The owner came up, catching me slightly off-guard.

"Well, hey there! Ya lookin' for one to roast?"

"Oh no. I know this sounds crazy, but I really was just hoping to hang out with them and ask you how clean they really are. I hear they make great pets, so I was considering eventually saving one from slaughter."

He looked at me like I was insane, but he understood. He made it known that he believed nature gave us pigs to eat, not keep as pets but also answered all my questions. He also told me his pigs are humanely treated and slaughtered. I wasn't sure there was a "humane" way to basically lobotomize a pig and strip its corpse for meat, but okay.

I thank him for his time and turned to leave, mentioning I might be back for one for a holiday meal. I skimmed for cameras and didn't see any, which I found odd, but hey, if he didn't care about pigs being stolen, then I cared even less that I'd be dumping a body there.

Climbing into my Jeep, I giggled. This was, by no means, going to be easy, but it would be a nice challenge for my talents. I'd see how far I could physically push myself, along with my ability to not get blood everywhere. Like I said, fun. I loved a good challenge. I had so many ideas that would be challenging to pull off and I looked forward to each of them. One of them even included two kills at the same time. My life had no shortage of reasons or people to kill.

I drove home and, of course, got stuck in traffic. Always, always traffic headed south. I made the most of it by jamming out to anything good that came on satellite radio. I didn't like FM because I was constantly changing the station or there were commercials on every station I switched to. I got it, but for like three hundred dollars a year, I got no commercials. I was more than satisfied with that.

I pulled onto my street and backed into my driveway. I waved to the nosy neighbor who was the sole reason I'd never be able to have a pet goat in this house. She was so involved in everyone else's business, and admitted it, that it came as a shock to go to one of the meetings and she wasn't there. She was walking her dog whose name I could never remember, but she was a sweet little thing. I still preferred my cat; she didn't constantly make noise. Sure, she was an asshole, but not a noisy asshole.

I walked in the house, and she made a liar out of me. Screaming like she hadn't been fed in weeks. I shook my head and laughed at her, picking her up as I put my bag down. She screamed about that, too, so I held her in a way she couldn't escape, only shred my arm with her claws, which I was used to. Antibacterial soap was my best friend where Minion was concerned. Ever since I brought her home from the shelter. But she was so cute and sweet when she wanted to be, like a typical cat. I wanted another, but she wasn't having it.

Now that I'd checked out the livestock farm, all I needed was the rest of the supplies on my list. I'd pick them up at some point this week. I mean, I still had plenty of time. Sure, two weeks wasn't long in the grand scheme of things, but it sure was to me when it came to a kill. It was forever. I decided this week would be the week I picked up the supplies anyway because there was always the chance I'd get stupid and forget. That's why I had so many sticky notes everywhere.

I set Minion down and took her food out. She started screaming louder and circling like a dog who was ready to poop. I secretly hoped she'd make herself a little dizzy and face-plant in her food bowl. She didn't, and I felt bad for even hoping at all.

It was time to think about what I was going to eat for dinner. I opened the fridge and found leftover Chinese. I pulled it out and sniffed it, nearly vomiting. I poured it down the garbage disposal, rinsed and trashed the container. The only other things in my fridge were water, wine, and a few of those spiked seltzers. None of that was a suitable dinner. Okay, it was, but I wasn't dumb enough to mix the two. I'd done it once before to a nasty outcome.

I called for Chinese, and it was here in less than twenty minutes. I was a favorite customer of theirs, so waiting wasn't a thing for me. Sometimes I swore they had my order ready to go, I called so often. Just as I sat down to eat, my phone rang. Unknown again.

"You've got to be fucking kidding me. I thought I blocked these." I let it go to voice mail.

Twenty

WHOEVER IT WAS DIDN'T leave a message. I wasn't sure
if I should be happy about that or not. I was pissed,
though, because I knew I had blocked unknown callers.
I double-checked my settings before I called the service
provider to have them set the block, as well.

Most people weren't aware that you could do that.
But there was a lot your phone provider could do that
you probably didn't know about. The only reason I
knew was because my friend Danielle worked for one.
She'd told me more than I'd ever wanted to know about
what cell providers can do, and I had to say, a lot of it
was disturbing.

That's why I laughed at having Google as a cell phone
or service provider. They may refuse to give certain
information to the government, at least publicly, but
they collected every last piece of data they could get on
you.

I ate my dinner watching the second season of
Mindhunter. The guy who played Ed Kemper was
absolutely mesmerizing. Turned out he was also in *The
Umbrella Academy*, but I digressed. He was so chilling.
And the guy who played Charlie Manson? Ho-ly shit! He
was so much like the real man, I got the chills, and my

skin crawled, and my ears almost bled. My brain hurt to the point of needing migraine meds. It was insane.

I shut it off, put my food away, and went to bed. I couldn't believe a show—a show that I'd read the book it was based on—could do that to me. Then again, imagination and talented actors who actually looked like the real people had a way of fucking with your head. If you say no, you're a liar.

I listened to the silence as I lay there with my eyes closed, trying to focus on my breathing so I could fall asleep. My mind was running too fast and had nine million tabs open, and all I wanted was for it to take a small enough break so I could sleep. Finally, it stuttered, and I fell asleep.

Monday morning meant fewer than fourteen days, give or take, before I could go after Brody. That was foremost in my mind and annoying the hell out of me. I needed something else to focus on for a week or so.

It was so incredibly difficult to shift into another gear, particularly since I hadn't yet figured out where I was taking Brody's truck from. Plan change—I'd anonymously invite him mudding, hit him with ketamine, throw him into the plastic-covered cargo area of my Jeep, and take him to his house. No cameras, barely anyone to see anything. Okay, breathe out, Brit. I felt so much better. Now maybe I could focus on other things, like lunches with Julie to really catch up and maybe a girls' night, since the last time we had one was when I killed Alex.

When I got to the office, I sent a group text asking the girls what day that week or next would be good for them to have dinner. Julie called back to my office with her answer, but also responded in the text, so everyone else knew. Heather and Kristen responded next, followed by Danielle and Sarah. Fortunately, everyone agreed that Thursday would be best. Unfortunately, no one knew where we should go. As usual, I had the solution. It was convenient, and we were known there. I mentioned The Pub, and everyone sent back thumbs-up emoji or smiles. That was settled.

Now onto actual work. There really wasn't much left, as Julie had taken care of damn near all of it. She truly was perfect to run an office. I would admit I was selfish and didn't want to give her up, but I didn't want to hold her back, either. She deserved her own office and so much more.

The biggest thing I needed to worry about that time of year was scoping out insurance plans and such for the employees who qualified. I used an outsourcing company for that because I got the best deals from them. I had plenty of employees who qualified, and I contributed more generously than most employers. Maybe that was part of why I had such a good reputation among those seeking work.

The door dinged, a potential employee entering. I got up and closed my door so I could make the necessary phone call. The information for one specific insurance company was requested for about seven different plan options. I thanked my guy on the other end and had the email within minutes. I printed it out and put it all together in a folder to go over tomorrow.

It was four-something, and the person in the office needed to be interviewed, so I opened my door and Julie handed me everything I needed. I looked it over and nodded for the girl to come in and sit down. She was nothing special, but the interview went well, and I told her I'd call her in a day or two with placement info. She excitedly thanked me, shook my hand, and almost knocked over the chair when she turned to leave. It took all the strength I had not to laugh. I heard her say "bye" to Julie, waited for about five seconds after the door chimed her exit, then burst into hysterical laughter.

Julie came in asking what was so funny, so I told her. She shook her head and giggled, but I explained it was "one of those things you had to see." Then she got it.

When I was able to breathe again, we locked up the office and went our separate ways.

Twenty-One

I DECIDED I'D TRY to finish *Manhunter* tonight, along with my leftover Chinese. It was difficult, but I managed. How did something like a show about interviewing serial killers affect me so much? I *was* a serial killer, and I wasn't squeamish about it. I dreamed of the time when I'd get to slow-bleed someone to death or dismember someone, hell maybe even eat someone or scalp them… This was what I did.

I couldn't even go to Ben about why this show had gotten so far under my skin. I considered maybe it was that I had empathy for others. None of the killers who had been caught seemed to have any.

But I did. I had empathy for those I allowed around me. I mean, I had a cat and friends that I'd do anything for.

I don't think any of the other killers ever truly did. They seemed to know "love" in different ways, largely caused by mistreatment from parents. I hadn't endured any of that, which made my condition so mysterious, especially to me.

The next thing I knew, it was past my bedtime. How I knew was Minion sat on the floor staring at me, irritated and waiting for her before-bed treats. I petted her, apologized, and got the treats, then took myself to bed. She followed when she felt like it. That was her way. Either she was on my heels, trying to trip and kill me, or waiting until I was seconds from sleep before jumping on my pillow, expecting me to pick the blanket up for her to climb under. Tonight was the latter, But I was out cold before she even came up.

Each day seemed to move slower than the previous, slowly killing what patience I had that managed to survive. Sanity was another question altogether; it was long gone. Was I sane or not? I never really thought about it until the time came when I had to practice what I thought was too much patience.

I thought, again, about taking out one or two of Brody's friends. I wanted to so intensely, but it was too close to my plans for Brody, and even if I could take them out, it would show a pattern. And more kills so close together meant more chances of making a mistake, leaving something behind. It would put me one step closer to being caught.

Hell, I sometimes thought about killing Cody and other friends' significant others just to have more time with them myself. I knew it was cruel, and selfish didn't cover it. But I'd have been lying if I didn't say it crossed my mind on more than one occasion. Then again, sometimes my friends backpedaled so bad, I wanted to kill them. Or choke them. At the very least, I didn't appreciate being fucked with on that level. If I gave you my trust, I expected you to honor that. I thought that made sense; my friends expected the same. So I lied to them about being a killer. Or did I? Was omission really lying if they never even suspected? That was the central question.

I passed my time daydreaming and maybe wishing, one day, I'd find someone I could be with. You know, like that fictional serial killer I talked about earlier where the books and show diverged. Yeah, maybe one day that could be my life. But for now, the last thing I needed or wanted was something like Sweet pulled.

Who the hell did that, anyway? I never gave him a key, he *knew* I kept guns in the house, I never told him he was welcome at any time… What a fucking asshole. *Wow, Brit, breathe. He's in jail for a while. Calm down. Use this anger when you kill Brody.*

I could do that. I'd gotten pretty good at compartmentalizing, and when I couldn't, I'd distract myself as long as I could. Mostly, I'd jog or go to the gym and abuse my body, which is precisely what I wanted to do now. I did have gym clothes in my Jeep, so I told Julie I was out for the day and took off for the gym. I was so inexplicably mad over things I knew I had zero control over, and acknowledging that I couldn't control those things and moving past them wasn't helping. I needed the physical outlet. If he knew the truth, Ben would have quite a bit to say about these urges to punish myself, and others.

I practically threw my Jeep into park and bolted for the locker room to change. I came out and hit the machines, starting with the chest press. I worked my back and chest for about ten minutes each, then went to the leg press for another fifteen. Free weights, bench press, more machines; I did it all until I could barely move.

This was me and my anger. I lived like this because I had control issues I couldn't fix. I tried for years, through multiple therapists, and couldn't seem to get a good enough grasp on it. Sometimes I even scared myself with my anger, but it had been a while since the last episode. That was in college.

This next episode—I felt it coming like a freight train—would be unleashed on an unsuspecting Brody. Knowing I had this much physical prowess kept me in check as much as it could; I just hoped I could clean the entire mess I was about to make.

Twenty-Two

Finally. Today was the day. I'd lure Brody out to the mudhole in the dark and knock him out, throw him in my Jeep, and do my thing. It sounded so easy in my head, but the reality was heavy—figuratively and literally.

Well, I hoped today was the day. If that ketamine wasn't here yet, I'd have to reconfigure my plans, which meant more waiting. I *really* didn't want to wait anymore. I went to the pickup and found the package waiting for me and almost squealed with delight. It was like Christmas morning as a kid.

He must have had it overnighted or something, considering our crazy fast conversation about it just a few days ago. I remember him saying he missed me, and I promised to come out and visit. It lasted no longer than a minute or so, not that we expected anyone to be tracing the call—they were burner phones anyway—but he couldn't risk being heard by anyone he worked with. He'd be dishonorably discharged at a minimum, if he was lucky.

I silently thanked him and took the package. I felt around as much as I could, easily finding the vials and a few syringes. This was the final piece of taking Brody down. I scheduled the text message from the burner phone to Brody about meeting at the mudhole—knowing he was stupid enough to meet—and threw it in my bag until the time came to wipe it down and trash it. Every nerve ending in my body tingled with excitement, my brain almost numb. This was the feeling that led up to the bigger feelings of fulfillment that I longed for. If I could have killed more often, I would have. The dangers present—potentially leaving a trail for the cops, or worse, the FBI—were real and I those were lines I wasn't pushing.

I pushed boundaries, sure, but not the kind that could get me caught or killed. I knew my prey; I stalked them enough to predict their next moves or when they'd be going to the bathroom. It was my job to know these things if I wanted to properly execute my plans…and them. As much as I wanted to kill Brody's friends, too, that was too much, too soon. The FBI would've been here, and I'd have been on the run somewhere else. I liked it here for the most part, so being tailed or anything else wasn't necessarily something I wanted. The only tail I did want was Minion's in my face. The floof that she was, with her frizzy tail… That was okay.

I went shopping to pass the time until the sun set. I'd already picked up my supplies, but now I was at the mall, walking around, shopping for Julie's engagement party and a few new outfits for me. I kept everything I picked up for Julie and Cody in the closet of the guest room so Julie wouldn't know I'd been picking things up for them. I was happy for her happiness, and I treated my friends well. Just ask Heather and Kristen. When they'd gotten married, I practically furnished their new houses. I always did for them what I could. I did for my father what I could, too.

If there was anything I thought he needed, I took care of it. I paid for his health insurance and any other bills I could help with. He did everything for me; if it wasn't for him, I wouldn't have Passing Through. My mother was long out of the picture, and I didn't care. She hadn't deserved us. I checked my watch. It was time to go home and get ready for what was sure to be a bloody good time. I paid for what I had and left the mall.

When I got home, I threw all the bags on the bed in the guest room, event those containing my outfits. I'd sort through it all tomorrow. Tonight was all about clothes I could burn if they got too messy, which I most likely would do anyway, just to get rid of any evidence. I contemplated burning Brody's house down but realized that was too extreme. At least one neighbor would be home, I was sure. My plans didn't include neighbors or killing more than one person.

I changed, triple-checked my supplies, and loaded them in the back seat, carefully laid out in the bag so I had quick and easy access to the ketamine, syringes, duct tape and contractor bags. Then I went to Brody's house. When I got inside, I cut up the contractor bags and laid them on the floor, taped some to the walls, and tried, unsuccessfully, to tape them to the ceiling. I tried again and managed to get them half-up, mainly because of the lighting. I knew I'd have to clean something, and that was, after all, why I had extra peroxide with me. Once I was satisfied with my covering, I checked the burner to make sure the scheduled text sent. I went back to my Jeep and drove out to the meeting spot.

Brody was there when I got there, probably curious about who the anonymous person was wanting to "tumble in the mud." I laughed and killed the headlights. I sat there for a while, letting him sit and wonder as people came and went. The tension must have been killing him. No, that would be me; *I* would kill him. At long last, I was about to get my way. The only vehicles left were mine, me inside, and Brody's, him inside. I left my Jeep running as I got out and walked over to Brody's truck. He shut his off because it was loud and we wouldn't be able to talk above the noise.

He climbed down from the driver's seat, keys in hand. I motioned for him to arm it so we'd take my Jeep. He happily complied, and the horn sounded. I opened my rear driver's side door, pulling a syringe and sticking it into a vial of ketamine. After withdrawing a little over three cc's, I tested it. Brody stood with his back against the grille of my Jeep. So fucking classless. I came up next to him and before his eyes went huge with the realization of who had beckoned him, I stuck him min the thigh, full injecting all three cc's of ketamine in him. As he started to fall, I caught him as best as I could, hoisting him like a scarf around my neck. I managed to throw him into the rear cargo area, which I'd lined with contractor bags while I was at his house. Then I duct-taped his feet together, his wrists together, and his mouth.

"Sweet dreams, Brody. These will be your last. I hope they're enjoyable," I said as I closed the door.

Twenty-Three

HE WOKE UP ON the way back to his house, so I stuck him again before taking him into the house. I only needed him asleep long enough to get him inside and paralyzed enough so I could smack the hell out of him. I didn't know how, but I managed to carry his full weight into and through the house to the weight room. I dropped him on the floor. He landed with a floor-shaking boom. At least it wasn't loud enough to be heard outside the house.

He woke up a little when he banged his head on the floor. I stood over him smiling. He tried to yell, to move; he couldn't do anything but make noises and shimmy around. When he stopped long enough to look around, he saw black contractor bags covering almost every inch of the room.

I laughed. "Scared? You shouldn't be. This might hurt, but it won't last long. I promise."

I walked over to the A-frame weight holder he had next to the bench. I surveyed the different weights and decided on a ten-pound dumbbell. Brody made some kind of noise and squirmed and wriggled, desperately trying to get away, but he only looked like a worm on a slippery surface.

I laughed again. "You should really have had better gym etiquette."

I lifted the weight in my right hand as I said it and brought it down across his stupid face. The sound of bone crunching and shattering drowned his attempted cry for help. Blood poured from his nose and leaked from both ears.

I hit him again; this time one eye looked like it burst inside his head. Blood gushed from the socket, and his forehead started to cave in. I grabbed another contractor bag and more duct tape. I started to tape around his head but stopped halfway. He was still alive, and that simply wouldn't do. I wanted him to know he was being killed. I didn't want him to know he'd be eaten by pigs as a disposal method.

I beat him over and over until there was nothing but a puddle where his head should have been. It took a lot more contractor bags and duct tape than I had expected, but I finally got him all taped up and leakproof. Somehow, I got him into my Jeep; maybe his smashed head was a weight lifted. I went back inside to clean up—he even had a fireplace for me to burn everything then clean it up after dumping him in the pig pen. I made sure I cleaned the lighting and the areas I couldn't cover and everything else. That room looked like a cleaning person had been there by the time I left.

I drove his body to the livestock farm and literally backed my Jeep to the fence and pushed him out. His body hit the top piece of wood, knocking it from its place. I grunted and jumped out of the back, picking the piece of wood up and placing it back between the posts, narrowly missing a splinter sticking up looking to make my life hell. I closed the back door of my Jeep and hopped the fence, landing with a slopping noise in the mud, sliding right into Brody's lifeless body. I dragged him, hands in his armpits, behind the shed that served as a shelter for the pigs. The sloshing in the mud woke them, but they barely made noise. They came out to see what was going on.

Once I'd pulled the duct tape and contractor bags off Brody's neck and backed away slowly, the pigs started sniffing the body. Then they went at it like they hadn't eaten in a week. I have never been so simultaneously grossed out and intrigued in my entire life. I stood there, watching, in my own world, until the crunching and breaking of bones started. I had to get out of there at that point. The sound would haunt my dreams for at least a week. I'd always hated that noise. I once dated a guy whose kneecap wasn't really attached to anything and always remembered being woken in the middle of the night by bone against bone. I shivered, and the goosebumps formed.

I hopped back over the fence, changing my clothes in the dark, throwing the muddy ones on a contractor bag to burn once I got back to Brody's. I had a lot of plastic to burn, which wasn't the best idea, considering the chances for some of it to get stuck in the chimney. I decided I'd throw everything into more contractor bags—they're forty-two gallons; they hold a lot—and go back down to Ybor and burn it all down there. It was the safest place, and given the time, there wouldn't be many awake to see me.

Back at Brody's, I triple-checked, again, to make sure I'd cleaned everything, and even cleaned some things again. I couldn't be too careful where blood was concerned. If the cops came looking for signs of foul play, I didn't want them to find any. As it stood, it looked like Brody up and left.

Once they found his truck, they'd probably suspect foul play again, but with no body—and maybe some luck—they'd again think he took off. How many people just up and left their lonely lives, anyway? Midlife crises were real, and maybe Brody had his at thirty-one. Even his friends and coworkers wouldn't suspect.

Honestly, no one knew about anyone else's midlife crisis unless it was that obvious. Some people hid it well, while other went and bought hookers and blow, or expensive cars and crashed them drunk. I've seen all kinds of things people did while being unsure of their lives. Age didn't seem to be much of a factor, either. People just sort of…did things and called them a midlife crisis, even if they were just thirty-one.

I drove the bags down to Ybor by the shop I'd used to kill Alex. I slowed down as I drove by, even pulling in the driveway and looking at it fondly. I'd use it again, I was sure, but it would be a while. No one knew this was where Alex was killed, and I wanted to keep it that way. I did have a lockpick set with me. I could leave the Jeep inside and walk the rest of the way to a fire pit to burn everything. I decided that's what I would do. People might see some blonde with a hat on walking with two big, black plastic bags, but they would still think I was just "one of them."

I picked the lock, remembering the first time I had, and opened the roll-up door. I killed the lights and backed the Jeep in. I hopped out, grabbed the bags, walked out, pulled the door back down, and put the lock back in place. It was like old times; okay, a few months earlier. There was an empty shopping cart nearby and no one around. Was the universe helping me? I wasn't about to question the good fortune and dropped the bags into the cart. Now I really fit in.

I pushed the cart a mile or so—I know, either a gutsy or stupid move—until I found a lit, deserted barrel. I dumped each bag slowly, not only so I didn't accidentally put the fire out by suffocating it but to make sure I got everything out. Then I dropped the empty bag in. The smoke was thick and black and choked me, but I'd survive. That's what I was: a survivor. At any and all costs. If anyone got in my way, they were dealt with. Usually harshly, though I did try my best not to kill them unless they deserved it.

Twenty-Four

I WENT BACK TO the abandoned shop after making sure everything was nothing more than smoke and ash. I stood there for a few minutes, reliving killing Alex here. Yes, it was true that serial killers returned to the scene. Those of us with brains, however, went months later, when no one suspected anything. I giggled and picked the lock. I left the door open to pull my Jeep out and rolled the door back down, locking it once more. I was sure I'd be back and was grateful that it was still abandoned and accessible.

The ride home was uneventful, but I was full. My senses tingled, and I was on cloud nine. It wasn't so much that I was happy, more of a sense of elation. I was high; there was no denying that. I always got high from the kill. Not like a sense of relief from ridding society from some piece of shit, but making my little piece of the world better for me and those in my immediate circle? Maybe.

The only reason I killed, that I was aware of, was because I liked it, and I didn't want to be surrounded by people like those I killed. Alex? Way too polite; nice kid, but ultimately intolerable. Brody? Well, I've spent how long telling you about him?

In truth, I was now contemplating killing one or both of his buddies. They were all disgusting and nasty. So impolite and inconsiderate. Bastards, all of them. If I could have gotten away with killing them, too, I would.

Sadly, that wouldn't be the case. Between going back to the scene, leaving evidence, and/or leaving a pattern, that's how other serial killers got caught. Plus, it was way too soon for another kill. I've said before I like to wait a few months. It confused local cops, and they let cases go. It was the FBI I might eventually have to worry about, but that was if any of them were astute enough to pick up on me. Yeah, it happened in a TV show, more fiction. My life was real, not fiction. The truth was that the FBI was stretched thin with most agents going after terrorists or kiddie-rapers, not that I cared why they were so short-handed. The odds were definitely in my favor, which was bad news for the douchebag community of Greater Tampa.

I got home, and it was dawn. I was still high so that after I fed an angry Minion, I went for my jog. Doubling the distance out from home effectively quadrupled the total distance and exhausted me. I showered and laid my head on my pillow, staring at the ceiling. I smiled thinking about how good it felt to beat Brody's brains out, quite literally. The cleanup sucked, but at least the room didn't look like anything had gone on in there that shouldn't have. I even made sure all the weights and the bench were cleaned. That was my final "fuck you" to Brody. Minion jumped up on my pillow, snuggled her way down on my hair, and we fell asleep.

I woke up around noon, which wasn't terrible, considering I'd fallen asleep after six. I brushed my teeth and continued back with my morning routine like nothing happened the night before. Then I went downstairs and started the coffee pot and grabbed the paper from the driveway. I sat on the couch with Minion, going through the ads until the coffee was finished. I poured a cup, added the requisite four ice cubes, and sipped. Today I wanted my coffee as black as what people would call my heart—if they knew what I was. I laughed to myself and sipped again, walking back to the couch to finish the ads with Minion. We put on the local news for no other reason than the weather, and once I'd gotten that fix, I put on a streaming service to start clearing things off my list.

I decided to watch two or three of each show just to get into them or decide they weren't for me. More than a few were disappointments. Things like that bothered me. My friends, too. We'd all talk about how they'd cancel good shows after three seasons to create utter garbage instead. And we all continued to pay for these services. There were a couple free ones, one in particular that offered fun shows like the original *Doctor Who* series. I decided to watch that, considering I'd managed to watch all of the new series in a matter of months. Honestly, I wasn't not sure why I have so many streaming channels given I only watch one or two and that's it. If I wanted to watch hockey or football, I went somewhere with friends.

My stomach made noise, and I looked at the clock. Oops. It was seven, so I figured I should eat something. I got up, Minion on my heels, to check the fridge for leftover Japanese.

Minion screamed as soon as I opened the door, so I grabbed her food and fed her, before going back to actually seeing what I had. There was some beef teriyaki, noodles, and I had some veggies in the freezer. I'd throw all that together for a meal. It was more than enough, anyway. I microwaved the noodles and veggies, then mixed them together. Next was the beef, which I added a spritz of water to in an effort to keep it from drying out. When it was done, I cut it up and tossed it with the veggie-and-noodle mix. I was delicious. I sat at the table, listening to *Doctor Who* while I ate.

I also thought back to last night. The feeling was incredible, and I intended to keep it up for as long as I was physically able. It sucked I needed a new plaything, but that's what happened when you broke into my house. I still didn't know if I'd ever forgive John for that. It was pretty fucked up. He could've been like a normal person and gone through my stuff when I was asleep, but no, he chose to be shot in my kitchen. Okay, it could have been any room, really. I guess the only difference would have been which gun I used. I struggled with the concept of forgive and forget. Maybe I'd try to forgive him, but it was too soon to tell if I could.

I rinsed my bowl and fork and put them in the dishwasher, along with everything else I used to make dinner. It wasn't a full load, and it wouldn't be anytime soon, so I put detergent in and ran it. Minion followed me back to the couch, jumping onto my lap. We watched a few more episodes before I decided to call it a night and shower and go to bed. Tonight, though, instead of white noise, I put that app back on and fell asleep to more *Doctor Who*. Forget visions of sugar plum faeries and all that crap, I had visions of Daleks and Robomen. My dreams were gloriously geeky, and I woke feeling happy and refreshed—until my cell phone rang.

Twenty-Five

I LOOKED AT THE screen. It was only Julie. I let out a sigh of relief and let it go to voice mail. She said she was already on her way in because she couldn't sleep and needed something to do. I thought back to Friday, trying to recall if she left anything undone to finish today and drew a blank. Something was wrong. Why else would she claim she had work to do? I jumped out of bed and got ready, morning jog be damned. I fed Minion, grabbed my bag, and took off out the front door, barely pausing to lock it. I threw my bag and shoes onto the passenger seat as I climbed in at started the engine. I took off to the office.

I knew it wasn't anything major; if it was, she would have just come over. She must have been stressed out about something. I hoped she and Cody were okay. I sped to the office as best as I could in the morning rush hour. I managed to get to the office before Julie and was opening the door as she pulled up. I could see the confusion on her face when she saw me. I went inside, shivered so hard it hurt, and turned the air down. I'd forgotten my sweater at home. Luckily, I always kept one at the office to cover my sleeve tattoos during meetings.

Julie came in and turned her computer on, then walked into my office.

"Why are you here so early," she asked.

"For you." I said, coming around the desk and hugging her.

"Aww, Brit, you didn't have to do that." She started crying on my shoulder. I ran my hand down the back of her head and back.

"It's okay," I said, trying to play cool. I hated that she was crying and I didn't know why. "Why don't we sit down, and you can tell me all about it?"

She nodded her head yes into my shoulder. I guided her to the chairs by my desk. I helped her sit before I sat down myself and handed her the box of tissues from my desk. She blew her nose and cried for a few minutes before even picking her head up to look at me. When she did, she burst into tears again.

"What happened?"

"We got into a huge fight about having kids after we get married."

"So, he doesn't want kids after marriage now?"

"He does, and so do I…" she trailed off and sniffled, blowing her nose again.

"Then what's the issue?"

"I went to the doctor last week, and so did he. You know, so we could both be tested to make sure we could even have kids. He's…incapable."

"Oh." I didn't know what else to say. I thought about maybe asking about adoption or maybe a donor—maybe he had a brother—but it didn't feel like the right time. "Do you really want to be here? I mean, don't you want to process this?"

"No, no. I'm okay. Really. I didn't realize I'd break down like this when I saw you. You've become more than just my boss, Brit, and I love you. I can talk to you about anything, and I just… Honestly, I'm fine. I can work. I thought I needed distraction when I really just needed to talk to you."

"I get that. I sometimes have the same problem and can't figure out if I need to talk. If you want a therapist who isn't a client, I have a great one."

"Maybe," Julie said, running her fingers through her hair. She blew her nose one last time and stood up, straightening her clothes and self as she did. She smiled and went to her desk.

I sighed. I was glad I'd come in when I did. I knew something was off, and I had followed that instinct. Listening to Julie made me realize how needed I was—how much I could not allow myself to be caught.

A week and change went by, and I was still waiting for the news about Brody's truck being found without him or any sign of foul play. Maybe the cops considered it an abandoned vehicle and had it towed. What I didn't know was that Brody had taken two weeks' vacation. It would be a while before anyone realized he was actually missing. I figured another two weeks after his vacation the news would break that someone reported him missing, blah, blah, blah. More waiting. This time I had no in with the cops. Or did I? Could I use Officer Jones and his kindness to pluck the information out of him I needed?

Well, I sure couldn't do it at the moment. Then he would *know* something was going on, and clearly, I had to avoid that. Maybe I'd ask him but when the time was right. I supposed it was an option, in the future. For now, I had to stay calm and patient. Again with the patience nonsense. I figured I'd ask Ben about helping me work on it. I was like an ADHD patient when it came to patience, and having someone help me with it would definitely assist in my future endeavors.

I called Ben and made an appointment for him to help me work on this patience thing. I hated it, but what else could I do? It would serve me well to handle it properly, anyhow. I didn't see how it was considered a "virtue," but whatever, I needed to learn how to use it or whatever. not ignorant to what patience is, I just don't have any. It's as simple as that.

My first few appointments went well, and Ben gave me good tips on what to do and how to handle when I broke and lost any patience I built up. Distraction worked well enough, but not all the time. I felt angry a lot; I wished I'd done more research and stalking of Brody. I hadn't done my job well enough. Between that and impatience, it was easy to see why I was all fucked up mentally.

I was madder at myself than impatient; I felt like I had failed. All because I missed one detail. One *very important* detail—his goddamned *vacation*. That could have screwed me in so many ways; luckily, something was on my side enough that not knowing had no bearing on my ability to kill him or dispose of Brody's body.

Twenty-Six

A MONTH PASSED BEFORE anything broke about Brody being missing. The owner of the livestock farm found a bone fragment in the pig pen. It wasn't anything substantial enough to use forensically, but it was enough for him to call the cops. That was amusing for me; watching the cops basically run around in circles to the different forensic labs in a futile effort to get an identification on the bone fragment. Then they searched for Brody's truck and found it in the Pasco impound.

I'd have been lying if I didn't say watching the cops struggle didn't make me laugh. They were far from incompetent; I was just more competent. It was all over the news, and there was even some vigil down at the hospital Brody worked at. Imagine—a vigil for a douchebag.

At the gym, though, was a whole different feeling. Even the guys he worked out with didn't seem to care that he was missing. I found that a bit comforting. They'd said something about he'd been known to just take off and not say a word, let alone contact anyone ever again. Almost like creating new lives for himself.

That was more than helpful. They even told the cops that, or so they claimed. Regardless, no one suspected anything out of the ordinary. And I felt good about this one. Maybe overconfident. Probably overconfident. Then, I realized, definitely overconfident—when the cops showed up at the office one day. Officer Jones was kind enough to come in alone and ask to see me. I met him at the doorway to my office, shook his hand, and escorted him toward the desk. I closed the door behind us as we started talking.

Julie was worried.

"Britney, it's come to our attention that Brody Rogers worked for you before he became a nurse."

"Who?"

"Brody Rogers. The guy who's been all over the news. His employer reported him missing, but his friends say he's notorious for leaving town and starting a whole new life elsewhere, complete with a new identity."

"Then why are you here asking *me* about him?"

"We're just running down any and all possible leads. Doing our job, if that's what you want to call it. As far as I'm concerned, this case is closed, but the higher-ups want me to run down every possible anything. I'm wasting time, basically. But hey, it's nice to see you again. We could waste more time and catch up, if you want."

"Thanks, Officer, but I've got to get back to work. Let me pull his file and see what I've got." I pulled his file as promised and didn't find anything worthwhile, but I printed it for him so he could say he did his job.

He took the papers. "Thanks, Brit. I appreciate this. Now they'll see I did my due diligence, and that'll be the end of it. I'll try to give you a heads-up if they want me to come back."

"No problem. Anything I can do to help." We stood, shook hands, and I walked Jones out of the office. When I turned to go back into my office, Julie stopped me with a weird look.

"What?" I laughed.

"Tell me you're not banging him. And what the hell is going on? That's twice the cops have contacted you in, like, two or three months. Is everything okay?"

"Yeah. Apparently, guys who worked here at one point or another keep going missing or just abandoning their lives. The one they just asked about is known to uproot and not tell anyone. People are strange, what else can I say."

Julie laughed and agreed.

"You up for dinner tonight?" I asked her.

"Hell yeah! I just need to call Cody and let him know."

"Cool, want me to call the girls?"

"That would be nice. It's been a bit since we've all been together."

"You got it, Jules. I'll make it happen."

I went back to my desk and messaged the group. All the ladies were in. Outback at seven was the plan and we were all excited. Seems like everyone had news to share

Turns out everyone actually did have news to share. Danielle got a promotion, Sarah's great aunt died and left her a shitload of money, Kristen's daughter started

kindergarten, and Heather finally got approved to start her own physical therapy practice—the bank approved her loan application. So it really was a celebration.

Julie felt so much better about Cody at this point, and I was all too happy for everyone. I ordered two bottles of red for all of us—and dessert—to celebrate. I had my own happy news, but I wasn't about to shout that I wasn't a suspect in a murder I committed. That wouldn't only ruin the night; that would be my confession. No thanks. I wasn't not about to go to prison.

We enjoyed the rest of the night with conversation, wine, and cheesecake. I was surrounded by my friends, and that was all I cared about. Good people and good times made better by good news. I almost wished I had some of my own to share, but on top of not admitting anything, I also didn't want to take away from anyone else's joy.

We all worked so hard for our accomplishments—some of the girls harder than others—and I respected that. We were fierce women who worked hard for our families, too. In my case, I worked hard for myself, my cat, and my father. I had no siblings that I knew of and, thankfully, no children. I honestly had no desire to have children. I preferred animals, cats particularly.

Then there was Minion. She depended on me like I depended on her. We had an almost dangerous codependency. If I ever told Ben about my weird relationship with my cat, we'd be told that we needed time apart and hug-me jackets and medication and who knows what else. Then I found myself excited to go home to her. At least I could share my good news with her and only her.

We finished out celebrations, paid out our checks, and said our goodbyes. We promised to get together again soon, but given the time of year, school would be starting back soon for the kids, so we may have had to wait until October. I was sort of okay with that. I knew I could spend time with each of my friends individually if we wanted, and we probably would; impromptu wine and movie nights seemed to be our thing, as a group but separately. I thought about these things on the way home and smiled. I led a truly fulfilled life. How many other people could say that?

Twenty-Seven

MINION COULDN'T HAVE BEEN happier that I was home. I picked her up and snuggled her to my face before she nipped at my nose. I set her down and fed her then went upstairs to change.

I came back down just as she was tearing up the stairs. She looked at me and flipped a 180, using her back feet for leverage against the wall, propelling herself nearly down to the bottom. She managed to grab hold of a stair and stop. I laughed so hard I about fell down with her.

When I stopped laughing, I picked her up and snuggled her against my face again, completely against her will. She tried to get out, and I was acting like that redhead girl from the cartoons so long ago who squished animals in hugs and said something about loving, cherishing, and squeezing them. Minion finally bit me hard enough to draw blood, and I let her go.

She jumped onto the couch and screamed at me. I sat with her and asked how her day went. Then I told her about mine, and we watched some shows together. Before I knew it, we were cuddled on the couch, fast asleep.

I woke before the sun rose, picked Minion up, and took her to bed. I texted Julie that I wouldn't be in, and surprisingly, she didn't ask why. Knowing her, she thought I was probably annoyed by the cops and decided to take the day off to work out and abuse my body.

That thought wasn't far off. I did want to abuse my body but more because I knew I was going to be bored for the next few months, which was infuriating. Maybe I'd pick up a new hobby or something. Or I could spend time at the range. That could actually work out, though. I did have a list of guns I'd like to shoot and eventually keep at home. Which also meant a bigger safe. Again, not a problem. I was comfortable with all of the above.

Granted, the range wasn't physical abuse, but it did help me concentrate and focus. So, there was that upside. There was never anything wrong with learning proper weapon control. Maybe I'd take up a martial art instead. Who knew? I'd always wanted to take krav maga, and there was a studio over at the Jewish Community Center, so that could definitely be a viable option. Maybe I'd call the owner and see about individual lessons. I had an issue with group classes for things like that.

I really thought about opening another office, but with all that had been going on lately, I still didn't think it was a possibility yet. I wasn't handing another office over if I wasn't not around. I really wanted to take a small sabbatical. I needed to get my shit together. I didn't do all my research this last time, and that was unacceptable. I couldn't afford slip-ups like that. I needed to get my head back in the game. I doubted there was such a thing as a serial killer retreat, but maybe one of those relaxation retreats in some beautiful country could work.

Or maybe a three-month stay in a monastery with some monks or something to help with focus and patience. I did some searching online and found a three-month study program in China. It sounded like a great thing for me. I'd learn a lot of things I needed to, like patience and focus. I'd do some more research on the program, but it was looking like I'd book for as soon as I could. I was still mad about dropping the ball on Brody's vacation time.

I couldn't believe I'd been so sloppy. I strove for perfection when it came to stalking and killing because I didn't want to be caught. I didn't want to let my father down by letting him know who—what—I really was. It would kill him. Osten, too. And who knew who else would be hurt by my getting caught.

My killing hurt fewer people; I killed those who were bad for the world and who didn't really have anyone who would miss them…mostly. Brody apparently had no family, and Alex's parents didn't seem to care. And those before them, well…we won't talk about the past. That's why it was called the past.

I went downstairs and grabbed my laptop and charger and fed Minion. I researched that three-month study with monks all day and decided I needed a passport. How I'd never gotten one before now was lost on me, but I needed one. This break from real life would be good for me on so many levels. I called Ben and canceled my appointment but ran the idea of the three months in China by him, and he agreed it would be good for me. So that was it. I was going to China for three months. For a killer who meticulously planned her life, when I was sad or stressed I could be a little spontaneous. Three months in China would be putting that mildly. Ben had also taught me that I was a legendary overcompensator.

I'd decided on China and monks because they intrigued me in the moment that I'd decided I truly needed to work on my patience. I couldn't think of a better way to learn it—or better people to learn from.

I had a lot to get set up before then. Mainly who would care for Minion while I was gone. She liked Julie, so I hoped that would work out. If not, I'd have to hire a sitter of sorts. Minion couldn't be trusted to be alone for that long with me having someone stop by twice daily to feed her; she was mischievous and would get into shit and break things. I'd left her alone once for a week and came back to shredded curtains, two broken vases, and a smashed coffee pot. I still had no idea how she pulled that off, either, given the pot was safely in its spot in the maker.

I texted Julie and asked her to come over after work. She, of course, responded yes. I showered and made myself look human and ate lunch. When Julie showed up, she brought Thai takeout for dinner. Damn, I loved that girl. She knew me so well.

I let her know my plans, from the passport down to China for three months. Even she thought it was a good idea.

"Well, you *have* been a bit out of sorts lately."

"And you never mentioned it, why?" I asked, a little shocked.

"You were so easily agitated; I didn't want to make it worse."

I nodded. "Makes sense. I was pretty…off, wasn't I? Damn."

We laughed and enjoyed our dinner. Julie agreed to stay for the three months I was away. I offered to pay her for it, since it wasn't in her job description, and she wouldn't hear of it. I was going to pay her whether she wanted me to or not. She was doing me a huge favor.

Then I realized something—she didn't want money because she was my friend, and this was what friends did for each other. Wow, I must have been off. I decided to apply for the passport the next morning and get that process started, along with booking my trip to China.

Twenty-Eight

I DID ALL THE research I could on this retreat. How I found it in the first place was silly. I just searched for "training with monks," and it came up. The fact that it was only three months compared to other programs that were two years and more caught my attention. I figured it was some type of touristy scam thing.

Then I clicked the link. It was really all right, so I started reading reviews and about the program itself. Some of the reviews mentioned the food was bad, but the program talked about how the meals were "prepared following the Yin and Yang Principles" and that they incorporated all kinds of taste, flavor, and holistic approaches into the meals. They even had Wi-Fi. Well, I found that a bit disturbing, but I understood why it was there. There were businesspeople who went there, and, I mean, I *did*, find them online, so it only made sense. Even pious Chinese monks had to step into the twenty-first century.

The site listed something like six instructors; only four were masters or close to it. They taught six different styles of martial arts, all at the beginner level, which was amazing. I was so excited, I couldn't wait to receive my passport.

I had a feeling deep in what I thought was my soul that it was a place I could find peace and calm and patience, finally. Hell, the reviews said I'd even lose a little weight. Not that I needed to, but I'd be more toned than I already was.

And I'd be more limber. Limber was good for a lot of different reasons: avoiding someone fighting back when I tried to knock them out, awkward positioning transporting them, or simply moving them in tight spaces. There were a lot of other things I thought about with killing and how being literally more flexible would help.

Then there was the strength training. After Brody's giant ass, I could definitely use some of that. Especially without bulking my body up. I didn't think bigger muscles would be something I needed, let alone wanted.

The more I read about this program, the more I wanted to tell everyone about it. But I was also the type who wouldn't recommend anything unless I'd done it myself. The program alone was pricey, and then I had to worry about the uniform, training shoes, flights, and transportation to and from the monastery. Regardless, I knew this would be money well spent.

I booked for two months out; that way, I'd have time to get things together before leaving for three more. I set an alert on my flight app for cheaper flights, and that was that. At least for today. Minion and I were exhausted—me from excitement, her from being a cat—so we went to bed early. Tomorrow would start all of the preparations and the waiting for my passport to arrive. That was another reason I'd booked so far out. Those things took about a month or more to receive.

I changed back into my pajamas and washed my face, then crawled under the blankets, watching the sun set on the wall of my bedroom.

If I didn't enjoy jogging so early, I'd have smashed my alarm clock a long time ago. As it happened, I liked watching the tide fall back into the bay and the sun rise in the east, even when it blinded me, and I jog clear into people walking their dogs. I got to pet the dogs then, which was a huge bonus. Like most of my friends, I liked animals more than humans. Also, children more than adults. They were innocent until corrupted by adults or people. Animals were always innocent.

I preferred cats, like I said, because they were more independent, but I'd never say no to petting a dog. I was one of those people who asked to pet the dog instead of just reaching my hand out.

I guess you could say I was a supporter of Darwinism and survival of the fittest, which could have been an unconscious reason I want to spend three months with monks. I somehow felt lighter as I thought about my upcoming trip.

I started to let go a little of the paranoia and anger at myself about not knowing Brody had vacation planned then having to wait longer for someone to report him missing. Maybe I was just having anxiety because I dropped the ball on the research part, but this jog was helping. I also knew that I needed to be more careful next time.

I had no current plans on my next kill because I was too busy making plans to calm my mind before proceeding. I felt it was a good idea. I could get my head back in the game, or even deeper, and work better and maybe not as hard. I knew I needed to get my shit together before I killed again. Even if that was almost half a year before killing again.

The next time, I'd be more prepared; more than I'd ever been before. I daresay, I could, with the right training, become unstoppable. Okay, now I was just full of shit. Unstoppable, who was I kidding? I wasn't a pro sports player; I was a serial killer. We all eventually get stopped, one way or another. I preferred "another," like Zodiac: Retire from the killing game and maybe pop back up every so often or walk away…if I could. I wasn't sure I could walk away entirely like Zodiac had, though. In truth, I don't think he walked away fully, either. I think he still killed, just not in the same way he used to.

If he was still alive after all these years, he was done playing games with the cops and likely killed for kicks now. I killed for "humanitarian" reasons and making my life a bit better. I didn't play games with the cops because technology was too good and too pervasive now and the slightest misstep could have me locked up. Well, in my case, I'd be sentenced to the death penalty—Florida was a death-penalty state—and the last person executed wasn't that long ago.

I'd be lethally injected unless I chose the electric chair. Who the fuck *chose* that? The only reason I could possibly come up with was someone who thought the injection would fail and they'd die a long, painful death. At least with electrocution, it was quick and almost painless.

I walked back in my front door and fed Minion. I made some coffee and watched her happily chomping away on her kibble. How great it would be to be a cat. I could kill birds and not be looked at as a murderer. I wouldn't face jail time, news media, the death penalty…nothing.

Cats killed because that's what they did,. But wasn't that urge to kill part of human nature, too? If I had time to kill at work, I'd look into that. No one was going to arrest me for curiosity. I could go to the library and look it up, but why bother when it really was simple curiosity. I wanted to know how far back the *Homo sapiens* kill culture went, and I was going to find out.

Twenty-Nine

I GOT INTO THE office a little later than usual, but it wasn't a big thing. Julie informed me we had a slow schedule today unless things picked up and people came in. That wasn't likely given it was the end of summer and schools were starting back up. We might get a few spurts of new kids here and there looking for jobs, but that was about it. The end of summer was our slowest time, which made it perfect for me to conduct my research on prehistoric humans. Not that I had any desire to write a novella on the history of humans killing each other. Hell, it wasn't even any kind of history of warfare I was interested in. I wanted to know, simply put, how far back did the records go of humans killing each other for one reason or another.

Okay, I wanted to know more than that, but the gist of it was that simple. I could posit that humans had killed each other since "a time long ago" and for "reasons such as" and, really, I could write some kind of paper, but the research would be for me. It wasn't necessarily for ideas, but curious minds wanted to know, and mine was as curious as they came.

I mean, we never did find out why that fictional doctor ate people. That fourth book explained nothing and was terrible and rushed. It didn't say why he ate people, just what started it. The TV show that was made based around would have gone into it but never had the chance before it was canceled.

This also gave spark to thoughts about why cannibals existed. I decided to include that in my research, as well. If I was going to research people killing each other, I may as well throw cannibalism in there. Which led me to darker things like organ harvesting for the black market and such, but I would research those things at a later date. This kind of thinking bothered me but didn't. Yes, I was a serial killer, but all these dark thoughts, like organ harvesting, were disturbing to me. Even in movies, it bothered me. You know, the particular ones where the kids get auctioned off to be tortured and killed and that one where the friends go to Brazil and are kidnapped *specifically for organ harvesting*. Yeah, those gave me the goosebumps. One of them made me gag, too. And then there was that series of movies where people had to basically kill each other to get out of the places they were being held… I swallowed my vomit watching one of those after a meal in a friend's truck. So, yes, I did have a sense of right and wrong and could be squeamish at times from real horror. But what I did wasn't that. The way I saw things, I was performing a valuable public service.

In my office, I got to work with a basic search first and bookmarking sites I wanted to read and all that fun stuff. I wasn't finished by lunch but took the lunch break anyway. I was famished, and Julie picked up banh mi for us from the Vietnamese place around the corner. It was delicious, like always. This place had great food, and it wasn't that kind of lunch that was too heavy and made you tired or too light and you were still starving hours later. Wash it down with a Coke Zero, and I was set. I was also a huge fan of Coke Zero, so there's that.

After lunch, I went back to my research. There were so many sites and articles I wanted to read that I found myself still engrossed in searches at five. I thought about syncing my bookmarks but realized I didn't really want to do this at home. There I had plenty of things to do; here I was so bored I could gouge out my own eyes with paper clips. So, I made sure all my bookmarks were saved and backed up before shutting it down for the night.

At home, I didn't really break from my usual routine of eating dinner and feeding Minion and sitting on the couch catching up on my shows that had been neglected. I did manage to finish one show, which automatically made me look for new ones related to my research at work. I found some great stuff from the different history channels and some indie shows and documentaries. I almost let it get me excited, but I knew I wouldn't sleep if I did and I was already excited enough about going to China for three months, so it seemed like I'd only be making it worse. I shut the TV off and went to bed.

Every day was much like the one before it, but I was slowly making progress in my curiosity research. Some of the articles said the same things, while others went into rich detail, breaking down the chiefdoms of various groups and violence between clans. Ultimately, it looked like humans had been killing each other for hundreds of thousands of years—probably since the first hominid picked up a rock or a log and looked at his neighbor in anger. So, basically, since humans have been on Earth. That was actually kind of comforting to know. It surely wasn't the levels of today's violence, but something like 2 percent of the human population back then killed each other. Reasons all varied, be it over land, women, children, food; again, it was all the same as it is today. We just had better weapons than our ancestors.

Some articles posited that violence was ingrained in human DNA, which wouldn't have surprised me in the slightest. For example, I was more violent that Julie, but everyone had a limit to what they'd tolerate before they resorted to violence. I didn't want to know what hers was. Or any of my friends, really.

The phones didn't ring much; no one came in. I was so intrigued by the history lesson I was giving myself I didn't even notice Julie ask if I wanted lunch.

"Brit," she yelled, pulling me from my learning trance.

"Huh?" I sounded confused, like I'd been up for days and had no idea who or where I was.

"Do you want lunch?"

"Oh. Uh, yeah, I guess." I handed her forty dollars to either have it delivered or pick it up. I didn't specify what I wanted to eat, but Julie knew me well enough to know I'd try anything at least once.

She walked out to the reception area and made a call. The next thing I knew, there was a delivery person here and gone. Julie locked the door behind him and came into my office to eat and ask about what had me so caught up. I turned my computer screen toward her as she set my food in from of me. She looked a little grossed out, but when she read the headline, she calmed.

"Why are you reading that, anyway?"

"I was curious about how long humans have been killing each other. It seems like there's more bloodshed each year, and I wanted to know how long it's been going on. Did you know there are currently studies going on to see if violence is somehow in our genetic makeup? It's really cool stuff."

"That sounds a bit morbid, Brit, but that's who you are." She laughed.

"Thanks, I think." I laughed and ate my lunch, turning my screen back to the way I sit.

We finished our lunch talking about how bored we were, and Julie mentioned how much she'd hate being without me for the three months I would be in China. When I told her they had the internet, she almost choked on her food.

"But it's monks," she said, aghast. "Isn't that against their religion or something?"

"That was the way I had thought about it, too, when I found it. But if they're booking stays via the internet, it makes sense that they have it. I see it this way: I'll come back more relaxed and with a lot more patience. You know I have none now."

We both laughed.

Julie went back to her desk and I to my reading. I learned a lot of really interesting things about human violence since our inception. I wasn't quite ready for the violence in our DNA article when I clicked on it, and I was glad Julie reminded me it was time to leave. I could let the day's learning simmer tonight and come back ready for more tomorrow. It was almost like college all over again, except I was the one getting paid, not some school.

Thirty

I'D FINISHED READING ABOUT the history of human violence and warfare—warfare started about five thousand years ago—and was on to learning about cannibalism. I was still anxiously waiting for my passport and my flight date and was occupying my mind and time so I didn't do anything stupid. By stupid, I meant kill one of Brody's friends without the proper research—just kill the dude and leave his body wherever it fell. That kind of stupid. Those impulses were why I had order and structure in my life.

I started searching for reputable sites with articles on cannibalism and was surprised by how many there actually were. I bookmarked as many as I could while glancing over them before lunch. I'd gotten quite a bit of skimming in to know that cannibalism dates back about eight hundred thousand years ago, and there were still cannibal cultures today. Reasons for this differed, of course. I was feeling like I could write some kind of anthropological dissertation at that point, but there was absolutely no way I was going back to school. This kind of learning was all for me. I enjoyed the things others considered taboo. Besides, it gave me ideas and tips for the future. Maybe I'd try it sometime.

For now, just learning about it and that during World War II there was quite a bit of cannibalism that went on. It was interesting. I mean, what would you do if you were cut off from food? Your body can only live without food for three weeks.

The next thing I knew, the mail had shown up and was sitting on my desk. Julie was in and out, and I didn't even notice. Wow, I was that into reading, I supposed. On top of the mail pile was something from the State Department, and I made a high-pitched noise of excitement. I felt the package and knew. Opening it, I felt the joy of a child opening a gift. My passport had finally arrived. It was about a week earlier than expected, which was actually kind of perfect. Now I could accurately clothes-shop for my time in China.

It was time for new research. Not the kind I'd been doing to keep myself busy but the kind that would help me not look culturally ignorant and keep me feeling comfortable weather-wise. I looked up the location of the monastery and the months I'd be there. I needed to shop for clothes I barely needed here: sweaters and pants and a warm coat. At least stores here sold winter clothes. I wouldn't need a parka but definitely a warm coat, some sweaters, long-sleeve shirts, and the like. I'd be comfortable, and that was all I wanted.

The phones were dead, and we didn't have much else to do that couldn't wait, so I grabbed Julie to help me pick out some warmer gear for my trip. We went to the mall and to Old Navy. I knew I wouldn't wear this stuff longer than those three months, so I shopped cheap and comfortable. It might even be cool enough weather when I came back, since my return flight was scheduled for the end of January—the notorious "winter" of Florida. Really, it would be cold a few days, I might get use of my fireplace in, and that would be it. The humidity and mosquitoes would be back after me soon after. Yet I chose to stay here. Maybe one day I'd leave, but for now, it was only a retreat to teach me skills I underappreciated and needed to learn.

We spent hours in the store goofing off, having our own movie montages, and trying on different outfits we thought would work. Some did and some didn't. I bought a new coat, too. It was warm, comfortable, and had enough pockets to make me happy. I didn't care that it was a men's coat because it had pockets. Women's clothes lacked proper pockets, so I needed something that I could wear and carry the things I needed to if I went off to do touristy things. I planned to spend most of my free time meditating and learning patience, which the site said I could do. I could even physically train more. I wanted to do both and would have more than enough time.

We ate at the restaurant Cody worked at. He was, of course, working, when we got there. So, we sat at the bar and drank and ate. Cody filled me in on school and how close he was to graduation, then asked what all the "winter" gear was for. I told him about my trip and that I'd be gone for three months. He said that Julie told him something about it and that she'd be staying every so often so Minion didn't feel alone and abandoned. That drove a knife through my heart, and I almost cried. To think that my little Minion would think I abandoned her broke my heart.

But Julie was right to think that and one of the greatest friends I was lucky enough to have in my life to realize that. What kind of pet parent was I to not think that? I felt horrible.

Julie realized I dropped my head and put her arm around my shoulders. "You're not the terrible cat mom you're thinking you are."

"You read minds now? Guess that means I really need to give you a raise, huh." We giggled. She understood that I hadn't realized what my trip would do to Minion, but *she* had. *She* thought far enough and deep enough to know Minion would need a human every couple days. I was so grateful for that, I had no way to express it other than to hug her so tight she thought I'd squeeze the life out of her. I loosened my grip and cried a little on her shoulder before letting go completely.

We sat there almost until closing time, and I took Julie back to her car at the office and went home myself. I fed Minion and took my bags upstairs. When Minion came up, I picked her up and held her—against her will, like any other cat—and reassured her I'd be back, that I was only going away for a little while and Julie would come stay with her. She was pissed, the look in her eyes threatening to claw my face off, but I didn't care. She was the closest thing I had to a child—the only kind of child I wanted—and I didn't want her to feel like her mommy had just up and left her. I'd miss her like a lost limb.

I always joked about how codependent we were, but it wasn't really a joke. It was true. I firmly believed that she wouldn't have bonded with another human the way she had with me. I knew that said a lot about trust, but that made me wonder if she had murderous intentions, too. I'm sure cats thought, but did they think like humans? I guess that was just more research for me to do during my down time at work before I left. I really wanted to know what my cat was—and would be—feeling about my trip.

I wrote myself a sticky note and stuck it to my phone so I wouldn't lose it, then took my shoes off and cuddled Minion on the bed.

Thirty-One

THE NEXT MORNING, I realized I'd fallen asleep in my work clothes and had to laugh it off. Minion was, as usual, mad we had to wake up. I went about my routine, brushing, jogging, showering, and such. She yelled at me as I walked out the door, me yelling back that I love her and would see her in a few hours. Codependency was no game; she wanted me home for good. That wasn't going to happen. I loved her as much as I loved Joe Osten and my father…which reminded me I needed to tell Osten what my plans were.

I hurried to get ready for work, calling Osten as I did. Speakerphone was sometimes a great thing, and right now was one of those times. He answered on the second ring, sounding worried.

"Joe, there's nothing to worry about. Promise. I'm okay. Not that I need a reason to call, but I have one today. What are your lunch plans? I'd like to see you and catch up."

"I have plans with another surgeon, but I can reschedule those. You're more important. And you're sure everything is okay?"

"Yes, Joe." I laughed.

"All right then. Time and place?"

"I'll text you when I get to the office."

"Sounds good."

"Love you, Joe."

"Love you, Brit."

I tapped the button to hang up and went about finishing my makeup and hair. I was already prepped for frizz since I hadn't washed it this morning; a ponytail it would be.

When I was done, I ran downstairs, glad I kept heels by the door on a rack, picked a pair, and threw them in my purse. I tore out the door, looking at my watch, realizing how late I was. This whole killing-Brody thing had thrown me off. I wasn't about to ask Ben because of that whole duty-bound thing therapists have where they have to have you locked up and evaluated. I couldn't ask anyone. Not about the killing, anyway.

Right as I pulled into the parking lot, I realized I could ask Julie what she'd noticed the past few months and how off I'd been. Objective opinions were what I needed, and she was the one who saw me the most. I parked and ran in, still without shoes.

Julie started laughing the second I made it onto the tile floor. I looked down and saw how ridiculous I looked and laughed with her.

"Wow, I'm a mess!" We both laughed harder.

I walked to her desk and set my purse on it, taking out my shoes and slipping them on.

I looked myself down again, then looked at Julie. "Is that better?"

"Not much, but it'll do. You look like you ran out of fresh dry cleaning is all."

"And I don't have any meetings, right?"

Julie looked at my schedule for the day and made a face. I panicked. She laughed again.

"You're the worst," I said through laughter, taking my bag and walking into my office. I dropped into my chair at my desk and started looking up places to go eat with Joe. I wanted to go somewhere casual enough so he wouldn't think it really was some kind of awful news or anything else bad. I settled on the Cheesecake Factory. It was casual enough, and the food was good. Plus, they had healthy options for him. Whether he chose them or not was something else entirely. But I wasn't going to babysit him; he was a grown man, and if he wanted to have another heart attack, that was on him.

I texted Joe with time and place, like we agreed on. He responded with a simple "Ok".

I went back to work reading about cannibalism and how rare it was these days when Julie walked in, closing the door behind her.

"Officer Jones is here."

"I'm sorry, what? Did he say why?"

"No, but he's in street clothes."

"Aw, shit. You know what that means," I said as I rolled my eyes.

Julie laughed. "Do I let him in?"

"Yeah," I sighed, "may as well."

As she walked out, all I could think was how I could get in his good graces enough that he'd share information with me. I needed someone on the inside, and now that Sweet was in jail, I didn't have that anymore. I shook my head in disgust, still in disbelief that he'd go as far as he did. I wasn't sorry I shot him, and I didn't think I'd ever be.

I knew Jones wanted a date, but I couldn't do that. Just as I was trying to think of what to say, he walked in.

I stood to shake his hand and offered him a seat.

"Hey, Officer Jones! What brings you by today? Looks like you don't have work today," I half asked, half stated.

"I'm off. And please, call me Stewart. Or Stu. That's my name. I can't believe I never told you." His face reddened.

"No need to feel weird about not telling me. We were on a professional basis then, Stu. What can I do for you today? Is it something about John?"

"Nah, he's given up his cries of wolf because no one believes him. We've got real crime in this city, and him making shit up doesn't help anyone." He stopped and thought about what he'd say next; I could see it in his eyes. "Britney, I'd like to take you out for lunch sometime. That is, if you'll let me."

I smiled and blushed—I *always* blushed when someone asked me out; there was nothing I could do to stop it. I blushed whenever I felt another person had validated me in some way.

"Stu, I'd love to, but it's a little too soon after John to be dating anyone," I said gently.

"Oh! Oh my…that's not what I meant at all! I'm so sorry I gave you that impression."

I looked at him quizzically.

"I'm seeing someone. She's great! We're engaged, actually. Oh wow, I feel like a complete idiot now." He blushed and hung his head.

"No, I'm the one who should be sorry. That made me sound really conceited. Like I *expected* you to want to date me. Let's start over?"

"I'd like that." Stu cleared his throat and started again, "Brit, I'd like to take you out to lunch on a strictly platonic level sometime. Would that be all right with you?"

"Why yes, Stu, it would. I'd love to get to know each other better. Besides," I winked as I joked, "it doesn't hurt to have a friend on the force."

We both giggled, and I told him about my trip to China. We decided to make plans when I got back and the jet lag wore off. We hugged and he left.

I looked at the clock on my computer screen and realized I was going to be late to lunch. I grabbed my things and ran as best as I could in heels out of the office. Julie took great pleasure in watching that spectacle and, I admit, I've done the same to others. She locked the door behind me and disappeared.

I called Osten from the Bluetooth on the way there. I was driving like I was in a crowded race, trying to maneuver around everyone else to get into first place. Except there was no first place, just red light after red light. I used the valet when I arrived, trying to avoid being later. The hostess knew me and walked me over to where she'd sat Joe. He stood, and we hugged, kissing on the cheek. As I sat, I ordered a glass of merlot; Joe had water and a pinot grigio.

"So, what do you have to tell me," he asked.

I stuttered and stumbled. "What makes you think I have something to tell you? Why can't I simply want to have lunch and catch up? We haven't seen each other, or even talked, for months."

Joe laughed. "Because you don't call me last minute like this unless you have something on your mind or an employee to send me that I asked for."

He wasn't wrong. I had a habit of doing this to almost everyone close to me. It was just another thing to work on at the monastery, I supposed.

"Okay, fine. You're not wrong. I do want to know how you've been feeling, though, and what else has been going on with you. But since you asked, I've booked myself a three-month stay at a Shaolin monastery. I'll learn the patience I currently lack, strengthen my body and mind, and all kinds of other things I basically lack now. Including this silly-ass habit of calling last minute to tell you something over lunch." We laughed at that.

Then, Joe's face looked sincere. "I'm proud of you. So very proud of you. You've finally decided to do something for yourself. And it isn't just *something*; it's to help you grow as a person and make you a stronger woman than you already are, but in different ways."

My merlot arrived while I was telling him about the monastery, and we raised out glasses and clinked.

"To you becoming the woman you want to be," Joe said.

I smiled and we sipped.

Of course, Joe didn't stick to his diet, but he told me that since the heart attack, he had been trying to.

Hearing that made me happy. I knew his wife and kids didn't want to lose him. Well, his kids, anyway. We all knew his wife traveled to stay away from him, whether it was all charitable work or not. Their marriage had fallen apart years ago, and they just didn't want anyone to know. If anyone actually believed they were still together, they were fools.

I told Joe about John and how he'd broken into my house and I shot him. He couldn't believe I shot a cop, but I mean, it was only the man's foot, for fuck's sake. It wasn't like I aimed for the head and was a true shitty shot. My aim was good enough to be dangerous, and John found out the hard way.

Joe expressed his concern, but I let it be known he didn't need to be. I was fully capable of taking care of myself, and my trip to China gave new meaning to those words.

Thirty-Two

Joe and I parted ways by the valet, and I went back to the office.

Julie was on the phone when I walked in, so I waved and went back to my desk. I read a little more on cannibalism and found out that it was not so taboo and that humans weren't the only species who practiced it. There was a species of toads that, as tadpoles, ate their families to survive; it also helped them grow much faster. It made sense. Prehistoric humans were thought to have resorted to eating each other out of need for survival, too. Survival was everything.

I did my last bits of printing things out so I could read them on the plane—things about the monks and the training program itself—basically the website. It was nearing the end of the day, and I scheduled the rest of the week off to get everything together and organized. On my way out, Julie and I confirmed dinner at my house for that night, and I walked out to my Jeep to go home and shower.

After I'd showered, straightened up, cleaned, and organized everything I could, I pulled my luggage out of my closet and started cutting tags off the new clothes

I'd bought. I put everything in the washer when Julie walked in.

Her timing couldn't have been more perfect. I yelled "Hi" to her and found her in the kitchen when I came out of the laundry room. We hugged, and she pointed to the bag on the counter. It wasn't food; she'd done a little bit of frozen food shopping on her way here so she'd always have something to eat when she was here.

"Jules, I have a proposal for you."

"Um, why are you talking like that?"

"So, you know how much I'm not a fan of roommates, but I want to extend the invitation. If you want to, you and Cody are more than welcome to live here while you save for the wedding and to buy a house."

Julie was so shocked, she didn't speak for what felt like an eternity.

"We, uh, we… The house we're renting is, well… The owner told us he'd basically sell us the house in the next six months or so. I'd love to live with you, but it doesn't make sense to try to get used to living with someone while living with a friend. That makes sense, right?"

"I totally get it. Well, if you ever need to get away, know you're welcome here. Now, let's order a pizza and get started on the list of things left to get done before I leave."

I called our local favorite pizza joint and ordered us a large supreme Hawaiian along with mozzarella sticks. We both started salivating the second I hung up the phone then laughed about it, particularly because I was about to go vegetarian for three months.

We sat on the couch listing the things that would need to be done at my house while I was away. I didn't worry about the office since Julie had that well under control. I would only be a phone call away, if needed. The list had grown quite a bit longer than I anticipated when the doorbell rang.

I paid the pizza guy and took everything into the kitchen. Julie grabbed plates and napkins and set them on the table. She also grabbed the notepad and pen we were making the list on. While we happily munched away, we whittled away at the list, making it much shorter. The main things were to have someone here when the cleaning person Julie would set up came in to clean—likely Julie herself. And make sure Minion didn't destroy the house. I asked Julie if she wanted me to put a vacation hold on the mail, but she insisted she'd stop by at least every other day.

At that point, the only thing to really concern ourselves with was a courtesy patrol. Some police departments offered what they called a courtesy patrol for homeowners who requested them while on vacation. I knew city police were too busy for all that, so I asked Stu if he might be able to manage it a few days a week. He promised if he couldn't, he'd have someone else do it, every day.

That blew me away. He was way too nice to me, which made me naturally suspicious. But if he did believe John, then he'd make sure *he* was the one conducting the patrols. That thought eased my mind, even if only a little. I didn't know him well and didn't want to ask anyone else for fear of suspicion.

It was all settled, and Julie and I finished our dinner in peace and fun. We drank two bottles of wine, after which I wasn't about to let her leave. I gave her a set of my pajamas, and she crashed in the guest room. I always kept fresh towels and toiletries just in case. This was that *just in case* I was prepared for. Minion followed Julie to bed, making me a little jealous, but also making me feel a lot better about leaving for so long. She'd be in good hands.

I went to my own room and put on a cartoon movie I hadn't seen since I was a kid. I stayed up to watch it, not worrying about going into the office in the morning since I'd cleared off the rest of the week. My flight out was twenty-six hours, give or take, including three stops: Atlanta, Detroit, and Beijing. I wasn't a fan of long waits at airports, but I did enjoy exploring them. I had no desire to explore the Beijing airport only for fear of potential kidnapping. Okay, maybe I was ignorant to Beijing's possible danger, I'll admit that. It was nothing research couldn't fix. Honestly, there was not a whole lot that research couldn't fix. I never would have known about training at the monastery, for example, if I hadn't been researching retreats.

I was still wide awake when the movie ended, so I chose another. This time, it was another cartoon classic from my childhood. I was feeling restless, and I hoped if they made me bored enough, I'd fall asleep.

Man was I wrong. I was awake until the sun rose. Like every other night I didn't sleep, I doubled my jog and hoped that helped. It didn't. I was so high on endorphins, I couldn't think straight. Then I remembered I had some herbal tea that would help me sleep. If that didn't work, I was going for NyQuil or something. Luckily, after my shower and tea, I got a few hours' sleep in.

I woke with a start, remembering that I put all my clothes for my trip in the washer and never into the dryer. I slid down the stairs as I tried to run in socks and bumped into walls and corners on my way to the laundry room. I opened the door of the washer about an inch before a stench emitted. I slammed the door, turned it on and threw in some detergent and fabric softener to make sure it would be clean. By the time the washer sang its tune, I was running back to make sure I got everything into the dryer and some of the things laid out because I didn't trust they wouldn't shrink.

I felt better now that I'd gotten that handled. Given I'd originally forgotten that the laundry, I called Julie to make sure we got everything we needed to on the list. She confirmed we did and said if there was anything we forgot, she'd handle it as it came up. I was incredibly grateful for her. I knew my business, house, and fur-child were in good hands.

Cody was lucky to have her, too. She'd make a great mom like she made a great friend. Between her and the rest of my friends, I knew what true love felt like. Maybe not romantic true love, but I wasn't sure that something I wanted, needed, or was even capable of.

I cleaned and straightened the house some more while I waited for the dryer to finish. When it did, I took all the dry stuff upstairs and started to pack. Sneakers, slippers, pants, long-sleeve T-shirts, sweaters, pajamas, and anything else I knew I'd need.

I could buy things like toiletries there and maybe even towels. The monastery was just outside a city, so I was sure I could find anything I couldn't fit into one suitcase. I'd learned how to pack things easily from a Facebook group I was in about traveling. If I kept up trips like this, I'd probably invest in those packing cubes to really make life easier. This would do for now.

Not everything was in the suitcase by the time I was finished packing, and that was okay. I didn't leave for another two days, so I had time for the things that needed to dry flat. There was nothing else to do around the house, so I picked up a book I'd been trying to finish for quite some time and got lost in it. The next thing I knew, it was dark, and I was happy and satisfied with the book's ending. Then I opened my e-book app on my tablet and bought every other book in that series. I thought the author was a great writer, and I liked her style. Her main character was kind of a screwup and turned out endearing by the end of the book. The kind of underdog you rooted for. I hoped the series would be enough to get me through hours in airports and on planes.

If not, airports had bookstores, and I had this app I could buy books from, so I'd probably be sick of reading by the time I got back. Not that I expected I'd have much time for reading anyway, given my return month started the busy season for temps. I was looking forward to life again. Of course I thought about my next kill, but I hadn't the slightest clue of who or how or disposal. Again, I wasn't worried. I knew someone would flip my switch and I'd get to be my creative self.

Authors created fiction, painters created wondrous paintings, and me… Well, I created dead bodies in original, and ingenious, ways. Then there was the matter of disposal. I strove for innovation and perfection. Sometimes, certain ways had to be reused, but too far in the future for someone to recognize a pattern, unless they were like the homicide detective sister of the fictional serial killer/blood-spatter guy. Did cops like her really exist, though? I wasn't sure, but given human nature and how busy this particular department was, I didn't think it likely.

I ate some leftover pizza, had a glass of wine, and took my tablet to bed so I could fall asleep reading my new favorite underdog.

Thirty-Three

THE NEXT DAY, I checked the dryness of the laid-out clothes—they were ready to be packed. I took the clothes upstairs, Minion close on my heels, and pulled the suitcase onto the bed and opened it. Minion immediately jumped in and got comfortable. I folded and packed around her, but when I closed the bag, she didn't budge. I opened it again, and she picked her head up, glaring at me.

I felt like shit leaving my only child for three months, but I had to do this. Not just for me but for her, too. The more patient I grew, the more spoiled she'd be because I'd be able to wait longer between kills and such. She'd never understand, and that was okay.

I picked her up and held her close, kissing her before I put her down on the bed. She grumbled as I zipped the bag closed and stood it at the foot of the bed. I petted her, but she wasn't having it and took off downstairs. I sighed and tried not to cry. I didn't really know what to do with myself today other than to spoil and cuddle Minion. But now she was pissed at me, acting like a human teenager. There was only one option: force her to hang out with me. Okay, I'd bribe her with treats, to be more accurate.

The one day this cat wasn't all about Mommy was the day before Mommy left for a long time. Go figure. So, I called the girls for an impromptu get-together. They all said yes, and I went out to grab wine and snacks. When I got back, I parked in the garage so two of them could park in my driveway and the others could park up facing my house. I was fortunate enough to have a great location on a corner so I had a decent amount of parking for parties I rarely threw.

I was home three minutes when Danielle walked in, followed very closely by Heather. Julie, Sarah, and Kristen arrived in that order—Kristen last because that girl would be late for her own funeral. Everyone came with a bottle of wine and extra snacks. This was our last girls' night for three months, but we had a great one. We sat around reminiscing about how long we'd all known each other, the stupid shit we used to get ourselves into… Then came the realization that we'd all grown up and had everything we wanted in life.

All of us except me. I was the most business savvy, sure, but I was the most childish, too. We all agreed the growing I needed would be spurred by this trip. And then we all cried and hugged.

I wasn't letting anyone leave after drinking as much as we had; it was like a college dorm party, with two of us in my bed, someone on the couch, and the other two in the guest bed. It was a great night and I lay awake, staring at the ceiling all night thinking about it.

I was going to miss them something awful. But I'd be so preoccupied I wondered if I'd feel the pain of missing at all. Only time would tell, and I was more than okay with that. I had anger built up from nowhere I knew of, and the less of it I felt, the better. However,

I also realized I'd be forced to deal with those feelings during the meditation and other spiritual activities. I welcomed them with an open mind. I didn't want to grow up, but I needed to learn how to process feelings, be they good or bad.

I woke to the sound of the front door unlocking. Someone thought they were being slick. It wasn't Kristen; she was still snoring in my bed. I crept to the edge of the stairs to see Julie at the door.

"PSST!"

Julie jumped. I laughed. She turned around and glared at me.

"Why are you sneaking out?"

"Uh, because everyone else is asleep, duh."

"Not the right answer, smart-ass."

"Fine. Cody called and said he wanted to cuddle…"

"You could have just said that. Oh, while we're on the topic, not in my bed, dammit."

We laughed, and Julie opened the door, waving bye as she left. I sat there staring at the door when she came running back through it and up the stairs. She hugged me so tight I thought I might die.

"Oh, Brit! You've given me everything, and I'm going to miss you so much!"

Then came the waterworks, waking everyone else in the house. Somehow, six full-grown women fit in a group hug at the top of the stairs of a townhouse. Not that we were, in any way, comfortable, but we didn't care, either. This was an emotional moment for us. None of us would be the same when I returned, and we all knew it.

The ride to the airport was dull, but at least I got to see the lights over the bay. My flight was scheduled to leave around eleven at night. I checked in and checked my bag an hour before the flight boarded, having made it through security with ease. I supposed that was the best part of flying early in the morning or late at night. I sat and read the second book in that series I'd started a day or two ago.

The gate attendant called for a range of boarding passes, and I turned my tablet off and picked up my carry-on. Standing in line, I tapped my foot, a habit I'd had since I was a teenager. It wasn't just out of patience, but I was also nervous and bored. I got bored easily, so I was really hoping this training would help with that, too. I felt like everything was wrong with me and it all needed to be fixed—except my need to kill.

The gate attendant asked to see my boarding pass and passport, pulling me from my thoughts. I smiled and handed them to her. She looked at both, looked at me, smiled, and handed them back. She didn't wish me a nice flight or anything, but I wasn't bothered by that. It was stupid o'clock at night, and I knew I'd much rather be home sleeping, so I was sure she felt the same. I walked down the tunnel to the plane, and the flight attendant pointed me in the direction of first class. I normally flew coach unless it was on someone else's dime, but I decided to splurge. Maybe I'd even take a spa day while I was there. I'll bet with all the holistic medicine they practiced, it would be much healthier for my body, too.

I found my seat without any problems, put my bag under my seat even though I had access to the overhead compartment, and buckled my seatbelt. I was ready for takeoff long before we took off. I closed my eyes and tried to fall asleep, but the flight attendant asked me if I wanted a pillow and a blanket—obviously I said yes. She handed them to me, I thanked her, and got as comfortable as the seat would allow.

Then, they began the preflight briefing about the oxygen masks and all that. I would have started to fall asleep, but the plane took off, my ears filling uncomfortably and refusing to pop, no matter how hard I tried. I swallowed one last time as I was drifting off, that being the one that made my ears pop. I could sleep in as much comfort as I could muster.

What felt like minutes later, we were in Atlanta, deplaning for an hour layover. I went to the duty-free shop for a book or two, then the bar for a cocktail. I was exhausted, and it really didn't matter much to me what I drank, so I went with a pinot noir. It wasn't something I preferred to drink, but it was an airport and I was on my way to China and too tired to really think about what to drink. I nursed it so that I wouldn't keep drinking and get sick on the plane. I still had a layover in Detroit and another in Beijing. I wanted to be sober for my arrival in China because you never knew what to expect when you went to another country for the first time. Sure, people told me about it, but it was not the same as experiencing it for myself.

They called for my flight to Detroit to begin boarding, and I walked to the gate. I handed over my passport and boarding pass again—something I was sure I'd get used to—and got on the plane.

Suddenly, I found myself stuck in Detroit for almost three hours. I got drunk. No way around it. The airport smelled, and the people were meaner than Philly people. Finally, they called for boarding to Beijing, and I did my best to run. The gate was right where I was sitting, though, so running was useless. I boarded and immediately asked for a bottle of water, chugged it, asked for another, and passed out.

Beijing looked like the pictures, and the people were rude and standoffish. I was stuck here for another two hours. Man this four-stop flight was crazy, but it was the cheapest. Some of the prices for flights I saw made me stop breathing momentarily when I originally booked this trip. It killed me that travel from the US to literally anywhere, including within the US, was priced outrageously, yet when you were international and traveling to another country, it was so much cheaper. Sometimes capitalism made my head spin, but I wouldn't have Passing Through without it.

Last call for boarding, and I was on my way to Kunming Changshui International Airport. Finally. It had been a long twenty-something hours, and I just wanted to get to the monastery and begin my training. Even if I was stupid tired. I needed this like a runner needed hydration. I would soon be a better version of me; one I could be a little prouder of.

Thirty-Four

THE MONASTERY WAS GORGEOUS. I fought every urge to take photos like a tourist, yet they encouraged it, saying that it would help us recall our time here if things got rough back home and we needed to call upon our training. I related to that, so I took as many photos as I could.

We trained five days a week for up to eight hours a day. Some of us trained more when we were given the option. I was one of those. I loved every minute of honing my body and becoming one with my spirituality. I didn't realize meditation went that deep and felt so good. I would bring this back with me and either continue my tai chi training somewhere back home or pick up a new martial art.

There was one I talked about before, krav maga. It was Israeli and was what they used to train their army. I'd love to learn it. Maybe it would help more with the patience issue I still had. I knew it was just the beginning of my training here, but I was still super impatient, and I didn't get it. The monks told me it was all in the discipline and meditation, but I couldn't seem to connect with the part of myself that controlled it. Or my anger, for that matter.

For three months, I worked hard to gain control over my anger and patience issues. I did achieve an understanding of how to control them; it was the ability to control them that got me. Even the monks couldn't figure it out. Or maybe they did, and my time had run out. Maybe they knew there was no controlling it, and they knew what I was. I didn't know, but I did know it was almost time to leave.

A bunch of us decided to go to Kunming City for a fun group dinner before we left. It was a great time, and the food was even better. Most everyone made lifelong connections with fellow students. I wasn't one.

I did, however, make a lifelong connection with one of the monks. He was the only one who saw the darkness in me for what it was. And he didn't judge me for it. He told me to come back whenever I wanted. He said he had someone for me to meet, someone else as dark as me.

But I didn't want a partner in killing. I didn't want to know another real-life killer. I knew myself, and that was more than enough for me.

I thanked him for his generous offer and said I'd think about it. It was getting dangerously close to the time the taxi would be here to take me to the airport. I finished packing my things, said my goodbyes, and went down to the waiting taxi. We drove in silence, the driver saying nothing more than hello and goodbye. I went to the gate to check in for my departure.

I felt like someone else here. Someone I wasn't comfortable with. I boarded the plane to Beijing and began the long journey home. At least I had plenty of reading to occupy my mind when I wasn't sleeping.

After another twenty-six hours in a series of planes and airports, I landed in Tampa just before midnight, and I was beat. Holy fucking jet lag, man. I was so thankful my driver helped me with my luggage and even helped me to my front door. I tipped her well and went inside. I barely made it to the couch and face-planted into a pillow.

I think Minion came and curled up on my back before I dozed off; I wasn't sure. What I was sure of was when I woke up at six in the evening, I was still groggy and grumpy. Julie was there to greet me, and she had food and beverages. Damn, I loved this girl.

"Hey, Brit. How are you feeling?"

"About as bad as I look," I mumbled.

She laughed.

"I've got a whole spread for us in the kitchen. Come on," she coaxed as she helped me off the couch.

I hugged her, grateful she was here.

"You don't have to be here, you know."

"Yeah, but I wanted to have things ready for you when you got home. I can only imagine how tired you still are. I took your bags upstairs for you, by the way."

"Jules, you're the best. You really do deserve a raise."

She blushed and denied it.

"Okay, if you won't take a raise based on pure amazingness, will you take one when we open the new office?"

"Well, sure, but…that's not happening yet, is it?"

"Oh hell no. I just want to make sure you won't fight me about taking more responsibility at work and earning that raise." I purposely said "at work" since she willingly acts as a personal assistant because she loves me. Weird, I knew, but I I'd have done the same thing if I had someone I worked for I loved so much.

I wobbled my way to the kitchen, smelling pizza, wings, and . . . was that stromboli? This girl knew the way to my heart. Spread across the table was everything I smelled and then some: fries, mozzarella sticks, even onion rings. There was beer and wine, too. I cried. I can't lie. I never thought I'd have an employee/friend who would do anything like this for me. I was a killer; a terrible human being, yet here I was being treated as though I was not.

We ate, and Jules filled me in on all the personal stuff I missed. She said work could wait until I came back in two weeks. I'd taken an extra week to recover and make sure I had clean clothes after the debacle of looking like I was a slummer right before I left.

She and Cody had adopted a dog they named "Applesauce." That was a cute name for a ginger dog. She showed me pictures, and I cooed over him. They didn't know what breed he was but he sure was cute. While we ate, we decided a girls' night would be in order at some point this week, too. Obviously, after I could keep my eyes open longer than ten minutes.

I started to fall asleep while eating, so I finished the three wings, two mozzarella sticks, and lone onion ring I had on my plate and went up to bed. My mouth had a nasty aftertaste, so I chugged a beer. It helped in more ways than one. I shuffled my way upstairs, and Julie helped me into bed. I thanked her and was out cold before finishing the word "you."

I woke up a bunch of times throughout the night and finally for good around nine in the morning. I felt somewhat refreshed and went about my morning routine, minus the jog. I didn't feel *that* good yet. Downstairs, I found Julie sitting on the couch watching some streaming show, sipping coffee.

"I made a pot for us, and breakfast is on its way," she said as I dragged ass to the kitchen. I poured myself some coffee, added my cubes, and joined Julie on the couch.

"What was that you said about breakfast," I asked as the doorbell rang.

Julie got up and practically ran to the door. Cody, all smiles, was there to greet her with a huge IHOP bag in his hand. I set my coffee down and ran to grab the bag while Julie hugged him and called him "the best fiancé in the world."

I laughed and set the bag on the table, taking out boxes containing French toast, hash browns, scrambled eggs, bacon, sausage, and ham. I nearly drooled smelling all of it. Julie grabbed plates and silverware for us, and we all sat down to eat. We talked about my trip and the things I learned, and Cody mentioned he was graduating in a few months and would love if I came. Through mouthfuls of hash browns and eggs, I told him I would be there.

We ate everything Cody brought in record time. I went upstairs to get some things together for laundry and brought them back down. They cleaned up while I started the laundry. The plan was, since I wouldn't need these clothes, to donate them to the homeless shelters. They just needed to be clean first. When I came out of the laundry room, Julie was kissing Cody goodbye. She wanted to stay with me for a few more minutes—make sure I was settled in, I supposed. I was more than okay with that. We talked for, maybe, five more minutes, then she left, too. I waited until the washer was done and the clothes were drying the way they should be before I went up to bed to sleep until the next morning.

Thirty-Five

JET LAG SUCKED ASS after a trip like that, but I was finally awake and myself again. After my morning routine, I went for a jog. Damn, it felt good to be feeling human again. I did feel lighter, like maybe I actually did learn something about how to control, or begin to control, certain feelings.

Then someone walking their dog wasn't paying attention and walked clear into me. My jogging knocked them over, and this dude had the balls to be mad at *me*. We argued, and I went on my way. I didn't want to spend any more time uselessly arguing with some dickhead.

I got home, showered, and texted the girls for an impromptu girls' night. Everyone responded when they could—they were all working—but the answer was still yes. I had things to handle now that I was home, but then I remembered Julie took care of canceling the cleaning service and everything else yesterday. So, really, I only had to take the clothes down to the shelter, which is exactly what I did.

The Salvation Army wasn't far, but I preferred to donate to a place where the clothes wouldn't be put up for sale but rather given directly to the homeless.

The shelter was closer to downtown, and traffic was surprisingly light. I made it there in no time. Dropping off the clothes was a bit of a hassle because they wanted to give me tax documentation that I really didn't care about. I didn't donate things like clothes for the tax deduction; I did it because I'd rather see them put to use than trashed.

I went home and relaxed on the couch with Minion trying to finish watching certain shows while we passed the time until meeting at The Pub. I must have fallen asleep because when I woke the clock read five p.m. Oops. I ran upstairs to put my makeup on and do my hair and put on some comfy jeans. I fed an unhappy Minion on my way out the door. Of course, since it was rush hour, getting to International Mall would take almost an hour, which was fine by me, but I knew Heather hated waiting. I also knew they'd give her our usual table.

I got there, and things weren't as I expected—at all. First, the hostess was new. Okay, I let that weird slide. The kid didn't know we were regulars, that this was basically our table when we came in. Heather stood, and we hugged, and I saw there was already a drink on the table. Second, our usual server was out sick, so we got stuck with some jackass who was… Well, awful was too nice a word. As the girls started arriving, I kept noticing a lot of noise coming from the private room next door. Clearly, no one bothered to tell Heather, or the rest of us, there was a party going on. I met the birthday girl and her sister in the bathroom, but that wasn't the weirdest part.

Our server took way too long getting us drinks and appetizers, so that already decreased his tip amount.

The party had gotten louder and included Asian music, which I was used to given my past three months. Well, these people had no respect for anyone else because even people at the bar downstairs started complaining about how loud they were.

When I went to the ladies' room, the sisters walked right into me, not apologizing or anything. Apparently, it was my fault they were looking down speaking not English. As they walked out, though, I heard them giggling and speaking perfect English without even the hint of an accent.

My favorite fictional serial killer had a saying about the rude, and as much as I wanted to say something to them, I let it slide. Then their party got louder, and I noticed they seemed to have no care for American culture; not them and not the rest of their party.

My friends were getting mad, and so was the entirety of the rest of the restaurant. We got our checks without even eating and decided to go to the place next door, Bar Louie, or something.

On my way out, I was racking my brain for the perfect word to describe the Asian sisters and their friends. Rude wasn't strong enough and I was still suffering jet lag stupidity. I pulled out my phone and opened the thesaurus, typing in "rude" and tapping Search. The perfect word came up, though I had to check the dictionary to make sure it was accurate enough. philistines. That's what that whole party was. A rude, culturally ignorant party of philistines.

Would I finally have an opportunity to kill two people at once? These girls were in for an entirely different kind of party. A party of pain and torture and suffering…

…and I was the hostess.

Acknowledgments

This book, let alone series, wouldn't be possible without the following people and references:

Practical Homicide Investigation (5th Edition) by way of a Thomas Harris acknowledgement. The FBI's *Serial Murder Multi-Disciplinary Perspectives for Investigators* Report (available free online), and *psychologytoday.com* for helping me add the necessary depth to Britney.

Ret. Sgt. Chuck Burns for his consultation where the textbook didn't answer specific questions.

Justin D., for helping me on ridiculously short notice with some nicknames.

Nathan, for his advice and invitations. I'm so very grateful I finally decided to take you up.

Mark…sweet Mark. Without you, I wouldn't be here. I love you more than I can express and always will.

Jason, for the awesome editing and blurbs and feedback and advice and just being you. You have made me the writer I am today. Let's not get arrested, please. At least not before we make that money.

Also by Amanda Byrd

13 Reasons for Murder:
Politeness Kills (#1)
Meathead (#2)
Philistines (#3)
Hungry (#4)
Bad Blood (#5)
Betrayal (#6)
Disillusioned (#7)
Harlot (#8) *2023*

The Morgan Davis Serials
The Girl at the Bottom of the Ocean (#1)
Before You Die (#2)

Anthologies
Thrill of the Hunt: Cabin Fever (Thrill of the Hunt
Anthology Book 6)